From the N

ASSIGNMENT: *Rec...*
diamond stolen on...
performance.

CONTACT: Ned Nickerson. *He wants Nancy on the case—to clear his new girlfriend.*

SUSPECTS: James Ellsworth, *managing director of the ballet company. It was his idea to use the diamond as a publicity stunt. Or was it really his elaborate plan to steal it?*

Ana Lokhar—*trusted representative of the Raja family. Does her secret romance with dancer Andre Bernarde have anything to do with the diamond's disappearance?*

Katya Alexandrovna—*undisputed star of the company. She was wearing the diamond when it was snatched. Could she be the thief?*

Belinda Morrison, *rising young ballerina and Ned's new flame. She'll let nothing sidetrack her career—and let no one come between her and Ned.*

COMPLICATIONS: *It's hard for Nancy to keep her mind on her work with Ned around. Nancy's new boyfriend, Brad Eastman, just can't take his place. And then there's the ominous figure in black, stalking Nancy's every move.*

Ra

THE NANCY DREW FILES™

Case 9

False Moves

Carolyn Keene

ARMADA

First published in the USA in 1987 by
Simon & Schuster Inc.
First published in Great Britain
in Armada in 1989
This edition 1990

Armada is an imprint of
the Children's Division, part of
the Collins Publishing Group,
8 Grafton Street, London W1X 3LA

Printed and bound in Great Britain by
William Collins Sons & Co. Ltd, Glasgow

FALSE MOVES

Chapter

One

SHE'S GORGEOUS!" NANCY Drew said unhappily to Hannah Gruen. "No wonder Ned's crazy about her." She nibbled on a handful of popcorn as she watched a young ballerina leap gracefully across her TV screen.

Hannah gave Nancy's arm a sympathetic pat. "I know how you must feel, Nancy," she said. "It's so awful to lose someone you love."

Nancy turned toward the gray-haired older woman seated next to her on the couch and tried to smile. She could see the concern in Hannah's expressive soft brown eyes. Hannah Gruen had

1

been the Drews' housekeeper and almost a second mother to Nancy since her natural mother had died years before. Hannah had bandaged Nancy's scraped knees when she was a kid, had seen her through the traumas of her junior high years, and had slowly become the confidante and advisor she was now.

But what could Hannah say right then? She couldn't bring Ned back.

"Hannah, I'm so—so jealous," Nancy admitted. "I hate feeling this way, but I can't stop myself." She bit her lip. "It was awful enough when Ned and I broke up. But it's worse now that he's going out with someone else." She turned back to the TV and watched Belinda Morrison, the talented young dancer Ned had started dating. Belinda was a soloist with the Chicago Ballet Theater, Chicago's top dance company.

Nancy was afraid she'd lost Ned forever to the elegant creature who had just executed three perfect pirouettes. Well, she admitted silently, she had no one to blame for the breakup with Ned but herself. He had been complaining for months that their relationship always came second to Nancy's work as an amateur detective. And, finally, when Nancy had been investigating a basketball scandal at Ned's college, she had actually suspected Ned of being involved for a little while. He had been deeply hurt by her accusation and said he needed to see other girls.

Even though she couldn't blame Ned for dating someone else, she still felt hurt and slightly angry. Especially since she was at home watching TV with only Hannah and a bowl of popcorn for company on a Sunday night.

"But it's not as if you haven't been dating," Hannah prodded softly. "What about Brad Eastman? He seems to really like you—and he's terrific looking."

Nancy frowned. "He's okay, but—"

"He's not Ned Nickerson," Hannah finished for her.

Nancy managed a weak laugh. "Hannah, you know me too well."

She studied the television screen as Belinda slowly stretched one perfect leg into the air. I hope she falls flat on her face, Nancy thought, hating herself for thinking it. But, of course, Belinda didn't fall. Instead she remained perfectly poised until her partner caught her and lifted her lightly into the air, her satiny pink skirt fluttering gently. The lights made her black hair shine as if it were silk, and her blue eyes looked radiantly happy. Nancy pushed back deeper into the living room couch, feeling completely miserable.

As Belinda and her handsome male partner glided offstage, the audience broke into enthusiastic applause. Then it was absolutely silent as another dancer burst onto the stage in one spectacular leap.

3

"Hannah!" Nancy said. "Here she is—finally. Katya Alexandrovna!" Nancy had wondered when the star ballerina would make her appearance. She was one of the world's finest dancers, and Nancy's favorite.

Nancy pushed the unpleasant thoughts of Belinda and Ned out of her mind and concentrated on Katya's dancing. "You know," she mused out loud, "I read that Katya has been having trouble with her ankle and that she's only going to dance this one last season. Then she's going to retire."

"Really?" Hannah exclaimed. "I can't tell anything's wrong."

Nancy couldn't, either. The dancer's movements were absolutely stunning! She spun into a series of turning jumps. She makes it look so easy, Nancy thought.

The skirt of the dancer's pink satin costume flowed gracefully as she pushed off into jump after dazzling jump. Her matching pink pointe shoes, carefully laced around her ankles, accentuated the muscled strength of her legs. And there, pinned to her bodice, was the Raja diamond! It was only because Katya was such a brilliant dancer that Nancy hadn't first noticed the pin with a diamond the size of a walnut in the center of her costume.

Nancy folded her long legs beneath herself. "Wow," she exclaimed to Hannah. "Katya Alexandrovna is incredible! I wish we were in the theater right now, watching her in person."

Nancy imagined herself relaxing in one of the plush velvet seats of the newly built Ballet Concert Hall. Her jeans and sweatshirt were instantly transformed in her mind into a flowing silk evening gown; her shoulder-length reddish blond hair swept up and held in place with jeweled combs. Hannah would be sitting on one side of her, and on the other would be Ned, smiling warmly and looking gorgeous in his favorite blue suit.

Hannah nodded. "It would be wonderful to be at the opening gala. And to see a brand-new dance choreographed for Katya Alexandrovna."

"The new pas de trois was written for Katya *and* for the jewel. I think they had the ballet commissioned just so they'd have to borrow India's most famous diamond. What sensational publicity!"

Nancy pushed herself out of the deep couch and checked the VCR to make sure it was running properly. Her father, well-known lawyer Carson Drew, was out that night, having dinner with a friend, and he had asked Nancy to make a tape of the performance so he could see it later. Nancy sat down again as Katya Alexandrovna was joined by Belinda and the young male dancer whose name was Andre Bernarde.

Andre lifted first Katya, then Belinda, then Katya again in a complicated pattern, which sped up until the two women seemed to be floating through the air as comfortably as birds.

Nancy knew that the steps they were doing weren't at all easy. She had taken ballet when she was younger, so she understood that even the simplest-appearing dances took long hours of practice to perform beautifully. And to think that Belinda's only eighteen—the same age as I am—and she's already a star!

Of course, the way Katya was flying around the stage, it was hard for Nancy to believe that she was so much older than Belinda! While thirty-eight wasn't exactly ancient for a ballet dancer, Katya's bad ankle in addition to her age must have been hard on her. But nothing stopped her. She was as good as she had ever been.

Belinda and Katya began a series of fast pirou-ettes, then Andre joined them in a stretchy, slow section. The lights began to fade as the ballet wound to a finish. When the theater was black, the auditorium exploded with applause. And at home Nancy and Hannah couldn't help but join in.

"Bravo," yelled someone in the theater.

"Encore," shouted another.

"That was beautiful," Nancy admitted in spite of her feelings.

"That brings this brilliant pas de trois to a dazzling close," the TV host announced. "The audience is thrilled, and frankly so am I."

The clapping gradually lessened and then

stopped because neither the lights on the stage nor those in the house had come on. The theater was in absolute darkness.

"Uh, there seems to be a minor technical difficulty in the theater," the television announcer continued.

The TV screen was still completely black, but the audio portion was working, and Nancy could hear the audience mumbling. Suddenly a piercing scream cut through the low murmur.

"Someone get some lights on!" a man, probably from the TV crew, shouted. A few seconds later the harsh stage lights did finally come on. The three dancers were still onstage. Andre, standing off to one side, was anxiously looking at his two partners. Belinda was kneeling in the center of the stage, a light shining directly on her, and in her arms Katya Alexandrovna was lying as if dead. The Raja diamond was conspicuously missing from the bodice of her costume.

"Oh, no," Hannah gasped. "Is she—is she dead?"

Nancy peered keenly at the ballet star, her eyes picking up a tiny fluttering of Katya's hand. "She's alive!" Nancy exclaimed. She let out her breath as, slowly, the dancer came to. A murmur of relief ran through the audience.

As Katya eased her eyes open, Nancy could see fear register across her face. Katya glanced quickly down at her costume to the place where the diamond pin should have been. There was only a tear in the pink satin now. For an instant she looked horrified, but quickly recovered her composure.

As Belinda started to help Katya to her feet, Andre rushed over to them. Supported by the two, Katya walked toward the wings, limping slightly and favoring her right leg. Her ankle must be acting up, Nancy realized. Poor Katya! Instead of her usual proud ballerina's posture, her head was slumped forward and the pink ribbon from her shoe trailed behind her right foot.

After Nancy knew that Katya hadn't been seriously hurt in the incident, she was struck with the full impact of what had just happened. "Someone's stolen the Raja diamond," she said to Hannah. "That pin is worth millions of dollars, and it's been snatched in front of thousands of people. Not just the theater audience and the guards who've been hired to keep an eye on it, but everyone who was watching the performance on TV!"

Nancy turned to Hannah, blankly. They had just witnessed one of the most daring robberies of the decade, she realized. And in spite of everything she knew about crimes and mystery solving, she had no idea how the thief had pulled it off.

Chapter

Two

THE NEXT MORNING Nancy flicked on the radio that stood by the table in the breakfast nook and took a bite of her whole wheat toast. A stream of pop music blared out before she could twist the tuner to a news station.

"Trying to get some information on the diamond that disappeared from the Chicago Ballet Theater performance last night?" Carson Drew asked with a knowing smile.

Nancy glanced at her father, looking surprised. "Uh-huh. How did you guess?"

Mr. Drew laughed. "Nancy, I can always tell

when you've changed from a normal, teenage daughter into River Heights's number one detective. There's a certain look on your face. And I know you well enough to know that you'd never pass up a chance to investigate an interesting case like this one."

"Oh, but I'm not investigating the robbery," Nancy insisted. "I'm just curious."

"It certainly is an unusual and daring crime," Mr. Drew commented, taking a sip of his coffee and folding back another page of his newspaper. As her father settled down to read, Nancy listened intently to the radio news report.

"City officials have voted to give themselves a twenty percent salary increase," the announcer was saying. "And last night, in a startling robbery, thieves stole the famous Raja diamond. The diamond was being worn in a dance created about the world's most famous jewel. The performance by the Chicago Ballet Theater was the first at the company's new home, the Ballet Concert Hall. The gem disappeared when the lights were out during a break between pieces."

Nancy scooped up a forkful of scrambled eggs, thinking hard. The thieves were professionals and smart, that much she knew. They had obviously planned the whole thing very carefully.

"The jewel was stolen from Katya Alexandrovna's costume," the announcer continued, "while she was onstage, waiting to take her curtain call! Since access to the backstage area was strictly controlled by security guards, police detectives believe that no one from the audience could have snatched the gem."

Hmm, Nancy thought, that means the thief has to be someone in the company. Now, how many dancers were there in the Chicago Ballet Theater? The article she had just read about the gala had said sixty.

The announcer continued, "The police searched every person who was in the wings during the robbery, but they found no sign of the diamond."

"Did you hear that, Dad?" Nancy asked. "This is some case."

"Believing that the jewel must be hidden somewhere backstage, Chief of Detectives Wilson has closed down the new theater temporarily. The Chicago Ballet Theater will have to perform in its old headquarters, which is right next door, until the new theater has been thoroughly searched.

"CBT's managing director is furious about this. He claims the company will lose thousands of dollars with every performance unless it can use the new and much larger facility.

Meanwhile, the family who lent the diamond is also furious. Karim Raja, head of the family who lent the diamond, spoke from his home in northern India, saying that he will sue CBT if the pin isn't found quickly."

Nancy took a few more bites of her scrambled eggs, but she was concentrating so hard on the radio that she barely tasted the food. The robbery could ruin the dance company if the diamond weren't found soon.

"CBT has been beset by other difficulties this year," the newscaster added. "There have been rumors of tension between the company's managing director, James Ellsworth, and its artistic director, Colby Baxter. A few weeks ago it was announced that Mr. Baxter will be leaving the company at the end of the season—his contract will not be renewed. In addition, the company will be losing its star. Katya Alexandrovna announced that she will be retiring at the end of the season. That's the news. I'm—"

Nancy clicked off the radio and sat quietly thinking for a moment.

"Do you have any ideas," Mr. Drew asked, "about who the thief could be?"

"Not a single one," Nancy answered. "There are sixty people in that company, and it could have been any one of them. It's confusing, that's all I know for sure." She shrugged. "Well, I'm not investigating it, so I suppose I shouldn't waste my time worrying about it." She turned back to her breakfast. Her eggs were cold by then, but she finished them anyway.

But she just couldn't push the robbery out of her mind. Of course, the thief could have been anyone in the dance company or anyone who was backstage during the performance the night before. But the lights hadn't been out all that long. So it was most likely that the thief was one of the dancers: Andre Bernarde, Katya Alexandrovna— or Belinda Morrison.

Part of Nancy wanted Belinda to be the thief. But another part of her wished that Belinda had nothing to do with robbery—for Ned's sake. That was the part of her that still loved her old boyfriend. A tiny frown creased her forehead.

Mr. Drew, who had been studying his daughter, put down his newspaper and reached over to touch her arm. "Hey, sweetheart, are you all right?"

Nancy smiled weakly at her father. She could never hide her feelings from him. Because her mother had died when Nancy was so young, she and her father shared a very special and close relationship. Except for Hannah, it had been just the two of them, so Mr. Drew had been both father and mother to his daughter.

"I'm okay, Dad," Nancy told him, hoping he would accept this without further questions.

Nancy had to remind herself that since the breakup with Ned her life hadn't really changed that much. She still had fun hanging out with her friends Bess and George, or spending an afternoon in the library researching old mystery cases, or riding her bike to her favorite lake outside

River Heights. She still enjoyed practicing karate each day—a skill that came in handy when she was on a particularly dangerous case. She still smiled at her next-door neighbor when she met her on the street. In fact, only the people in her life who knew her best would have noticed that anything was wrong.

But something was. Nancy was moping over Ned, and she hated herself for doing it. But she missed him and that was the simple truth. Even when she was with her new boyfriend, Brad Eastman, the pain of losing Ned did not go away.

The Drews' doorbell chimed, and Nancy ran to the front door. "I'll get it," she called. She pulled the door open.

"Ned!" Nancy cried in amazement. She had been daydreaming about him so much lately—his wavy brown hair, his loving dark eyes, his strong, athletic body—that she was surprised to find him standing in front of her in person.

"Hi, Nancy," Ned said, trying to sound casual. But she could tell by his tone that he wasn't feeling nearly so relaxed as he sounded. He stepped into the Drews' entryway. "Mind if I come in?"

"Of course not," Nancy answered quickly, shutting the door behind him. "Um—" she started, searching for something to say. "How've you been lately?"

"Okay. We've got a vacation from school this week. And since basketball season's over and I don't have to train, I can really take it easy and enjoy the vacation."

"That's nice," Nancy said, feeling uncomfortable. Ned had always spent his vacations from Emerson College with her. But things were different now, and she just had to accept that. "How did the end of the season go?"

Ned smiled, and a bittersweet sensation shot through Nancy. It had been so long since she had seen that sincere, shy expression on his handsome face. "We won our big game with Chicago U.—and I made the final basket."

Ned tried to act modest, but Nancy could tell how proud he was. She smiled back warmly. "Super. Everyone on campus must have gone crazy afterward. Emerson's been trying to beat Chicago for years."

"Yeah, and we finally did it," Ned said. There was a moment of awkward silence. "It's good to see you again," he said finally. His warm brown eyes briefly met Nancy's and revealed some of the emotion he was trying to hide.

"I'm glad you came, too," Nancy admitted.

"But to tell the truth," Ned said self-consciously, "I'm actually here on business." He hurried on before Nancy could get in a word. "You must have heard about the robbery at CBT last night. Well, they suspect Belinda. They didn't find the diamond on her when they searched her, but they still think she could have taken it and

15

hidden it! Anyway, she and Andre Bernarde are both being investigated. Katya Alexandrovna was hurt during the attack, so she's off the hook, at least for now."

"I see," Nancy said, trying not to show any emotion. "They must suspect Belinda because she was holding Katya when the lights came on."

Ned nodded. "But she didn't do it," he burst out. "She swore to me that she went over to Katya only *after* the scream. And now the company won't let her or Andre perform again until the diamond's found. They say it'll be bad publicity if the two main suspects dance!"

As Nancy listened to Ned, her heart began to sink. So he hadn't come to see her. It was only Belinda he cared about, and he merely thought Nancy could help his new girlfriend.

Ned continued, his voice filled with unhappiness and concern. "Nancy, if Belinda can't perform for a few weeks—or a few months, if the investigation takes a long time—it could seriously damage her career. She's been working hard to be a dancer all her life, and it would be terrible if things were ruined for her now. Especially when she didn't have anything to do with the robbery."

Nancy sighed unhappily. "So you want me to take on the case," she said slowly, "and prove that Belinda is innocent."

Her words brought such a big smile to Ned's

face that Nancy wished she hadn't spoken. "Nancy, would you?"

Nancy bit her lip. It hurt to see Ned so worried about another girl. And obviously, he didn't care how she felt if he asked her to solve a problem for his new girlfriend. The truth was, Nancy didn't want to help Belinda, not one tiny bit.

When they'd been going out, Ned had always complained when Nancy began a new mystery. He had been jealous of all the time she spent sleuthing. But now it didn't matter to him. He couldn't wait to get her started on another case.

But then, Nancy thought, this robbery could turn out to be a very big case for me. And if Ned could get her in on the case, shouldn't she jump at the chance?

Nancy felt torn. She wanted to say no to Ned. How could he decide to cool their relationship and start seeing someone else but then expect Nancy to be there for him whenever he needed her? Still, Nancy could never resist an interesting mystery when she came across one. In fact, that was the reason she and Ned had broken up in the first place.

Well, she shouldn't mess up a great opportunity for a new case just because of Ned, should she?

"Okay," she said. "I'll do it."

"Oh, Nancy!" Ned cried excitedly. He took a step toward her and spread his arms as if he were about to enfold her in a gigantic hug. But he stopped himself and dropped his arms quickly to his sides. "That's great—really terrific," he said.

Nancy looked down at the floor. Working on a case for Ned was going to be hard. But she'd have to ignore her personal feelings and just be professional about the investigation.

"There's one thing you have to understand, Ned," Nancy said carefully. "I'm going to be looking for the truth about this robbery. If I find any evidence *against* Belinda, there's no way I can hide it. Can you accept that?"

Ned smiled and his brown eyes lit up happily. "Of course, Nancy. I'd never ask you to lie. But, anyway, I'm not worried because I'm sure Belinda didn't do it."

Nancy bit her lip. Just as he'd been sure of his teammates' innocence during the basketball mystery Nancy had investigated at Emerson College? But she didn't mention it to Ned. "When can I start?" she asked simply.

"Right now!" Ned told her enthusiastically. "CBT has rehearsals all day to restage the dances for the old theater, which is so much smaller than the new one. All the dancers will be over there rehearsing. And because of the police order not to use the new theater, the crew is moving scenery and costumes back to the old house. It's a good thing that CBT still has all its administrative offices, shops, and storage areas in the old theater next door. Can you imagine the confusion if they had to move everything back? Since so much is going on, everyone you'll need to talk to will be there today."

"Great," Nancy said, starting to feel the familiar excitement of investigating a new case.

"I'm driving to CBT now. Why don't I give you a lift?"

"Okay. Let me get some stuff and tell my dad what's up."

Nancy ran up the stairs to her room and gathered together a few necessities—a pad and pen for making observations, a complete lock-picking kit, and a small bottle of chemical powder for preserving fingerprints.

She quickly ran a brush through her hair, then, on impulse, she added a gold heart-shaped necklace to her outfit. It matched her earrings and added a delicate touch to her bulky navy sweater. Ned had always liked that necklace.

Nancy ran downstairs and briefed her father about what was happening before hurrying back to the entryway.

"I'm glad you're coming with us now," Ned told her as he helped her into her jacket. "It'll give Belinda a chance to tell you what happened last night."

Belinda! Nancy stopped with her hand on the doorknob and wondered why Belinda would be in River Heights. Of course, she probably came out

19

early to talk to Ned about her problem. Why else would she be there?

Ignoring her feelings of jealousy, Nancy opened the front door. You're on a case now, she told herself. This is no time to get emotional.

As Nancy stepped into the chilly March wind, she saw Ned's car parked in the Drews' driveway. She walked purposefully toward it and, opening the door, got into the backseat. From the front passenger's seat, Belinda Morrison turned and stared at her curiously. She looked just as gorgeous as she had on TV the night before. Nancy leaned over to her, trying desperately to push back the flood of jealousy that threatened to overwhelm her. "Hi," she said casually.

Belinda smiled sweetly—maybe just a little too sweetly, Nancy decided. "So you're Nancy Drew, Ned's old girlfriend," she said. The word *old* stung Nancy. "I'm glad you've decided to help me out," Belinda continued. "My career is so important, and this silly diamond theft shouldn't get in the way of it—especially since I had nothing to do with it." She gave a light toss of her long, jet black hair. "Don't you agree?"

Nancy stared at Belinda in amazement. How selfish! The Chicago Ballet Theater was in big trouble over the missing diamond, but Belinda was only worried about herself.

Well, Belinda could say she was innocent, but Nancy hadn't crossed her off the suspect list. And she wouldn't until she had facts—hard facts—to prove the girl innocent.

I'm going to find out who's responsible for this crime, she said silently. And if it's you, Belinda Morrison, I'm going to make sure the entire city of Chicago finds out about it. Fast. And then what will happen to your precious career?

Chapter

Three

Nancy breathed more easily as soon as Ned pulled the car up in front of the massive white-stone building, which still housed CBT's offices, rehearsal studios, shops, and original theater.

The ride into the city with Ned and Belinda had been horrendous. Nancy knew it wasn't her own feelings that made her think that Belinda was snobby and self-centered. The dancer really was those things. And she hadn't shed any light on the Raja diamond theft, either.

Nancy glanced at Ned. Belinda was super-sweet to him, but Nancy knew it was all an act. How could he be taken in by it? How could he like this

22

conceited girl? Except for her looks, Nancy couldn't imagine what Ned saw in Belinda.

Nancy got out of the backseat, and Ned and Belinda followed her as they all walked into the CBT building.

"Well, here we are," Ned said. Tall, sculpted marble columns supported the high ceiling, and a wide, majestic flight of stairs led up to the second floor offices. A huge painting of a famous CBT dancer was hung on one wall.

"Ever since I've been coming to CBT performances, I've loved this place," Nancy commented. "But I've never seen anything but the lobby and the theater. What else is on this floor?"

"Just dressing rooms and backstage. The dance studios, costume storage room, costume shop, and the administrative offices are on the second floor. The whole third floor is for scenery construction and storage. There's a back stairway over there." Ned pointed behind them.

"Whom do I see to get started on the case?" Nancy wanted to know.

"James Ellsworth, CBT's managing director. He's friendly with Belinda, and I've gotten to know him recently. I called him early this morning and said you might be coming in."

Nancy unbuttoned her jacket and pulled it off. So Ned had told the managing director about her before he'd even asked her to investigate the crime. He had been so sure she'd say yes.

Nancy turned toward Belinda. "What's Mr. Ellsworth like?" she asked. "I should have a little background on him before we meet."

Belinda shrugged as if the subject didn't interest her much. "He's a nice guy. We get along pretty well. Of course, some people in the company don't like him. For instance, our artistic director, Colby Baxter. Those two have been feuding for years. Personally, I'm not all that fond of Colby. He's the one who won't let me dance until the diamond's found."

"That must be really hard on you," Nancy answered, trying to sound sympathetic. "And how does James Ellsworth feel about Colby Baxter?"

Belinda threw Nancy one of her all-too-sweet smiles. "You don't need to hear all this from me. The people in this company love to gossip almost as much as they love to dance. Just ask a few of the corps dancers, and they'll tell you the whole story."

Nancy's expression tightened. Great! Belinda was about as talkative as a brick wall. How was she going to get clues to the mystery if the dancer didn't open up to her?

Ned glanced quickly at Nancy. "Come on," he said, trying to smooth over the tense moment. "I'll take you to meet Mr. Ellsworth."

"Okay," Nancy said, feeling annoyed.

Belinda stepped closer to Ned. "I'm going to get

ready for ballet class before rehearsal. Why don't you come up later and watch?" She slipped her hands behind Ned's neck and planted a kiss on his lips, then she let a finger run slowly down his shoulder. "See you in a bit." She turned and ran lightly up the staircase.

Nancy caught her breath. It hurt to see another girl kiss Ned. It hurt a lot.

Ned glanced at Nancy, looking a little uncomfortable himself. Then he reached for her arm and guided her up the steps.

"When I talked to Mr. Ellsworth this morning," Ned commented, "he seemed happy to have you on the case. He figured, the more people working on it, the better. Especially after I told him what a great detective you are."

Nancy frowned. Go ahead, Ned, flatter me. It won't make the hurt go away.

"Anyway, Ellsworth is the money brain at CBT. He does all the fund-raising and he keeps the company in pointe shoes and costumes. It was his idea to create a ballet to use the Raja diamond. All done for publicity. He makes no decisions about the actual dancing."

"Who takes care of that?"

"That's the artistic director, Colby Baxter," Ned explained. "The dancers say both Baxter and Ellsworth are great at what they do, but they can't stand each other. A couple of times they've practically punched each other out," he finished.

Nancy smiled. "Sounds like some pair! I'll have to keep an eye on both of them."

"Could be explosive," Ned said, smiling, too.

He led Nancy into a large reception room. James Ellsworth's personal secretary took their jackets and said they could leave them with her for the rest of the day. Then she buzzed the managing director to announce them. "He's expecting you," she said after a moment. "Go right in."

"Okay," Ned told Nancy, "you're on your own now. I want to check out that ballet class."

"Sure," Nancy managed to say. So Ned was going to go watch Belinda jump around a dance studio in some skintight leotard. If only he'd stay with her. Suddenly she had an almost irresistible urge to slide her arms around Ned's neck and kiss him, just the way Belinda had.

Ned went to the door, then turned back to face Nancy. "Be careful," he said, real concern in his dark eyes. Then he hurried out of the reception room.

Nancy took a deep breath and swallowed hard. It was so confusing being with Ned. He still cared about her, that much she knew. But it was Belinda he loved, and that hurt very badly. Nancy's only consolation was Brad. Without him, she knew she'd feel completely alone.

Nancy smoothed her sweater and forced herself to smile at the secretary. Okay, time to turn off the feelings and become Nancy Drew, detective.

She pushed open the door to James Ellsworth's office and stepped inside.

The distinguished older man dressed in a perfectly tailored blue pin-striped suit was sitting behind a massive, carved oak desk. A silver pen set was placed at his right hand with a panel of telephone lines. Heavy drapes framed a perfect view of the Chicago skyline.

"Ms. Drew, I'm pleased you could come," James Ellsworth said, standing up behind his desk and extending his hand to Nancy.

"I'm glad to be here. This case sounds fascinating. And, of course, I'd like to help." She shook the managing director's hand and sat down opposite his desk on a soft white couch.

"The police have given us clearance to have private detectives work on the case, and the Raja family demands that we do. Even though you're very young, you have quite a reputation and we've all heard glowing reports about your work. So, we're very happy to have you here."

"Thanks," Nancy said, smiling. She ran a hand through her hair. "Please tell me what really happened last night. I saw the TV broadcast and I've heard the radio reports, but there are still a lot of unanswered questions."

"Well," James Ellsworth said, seated again in his cushioned swivel chair, "everything was going just fine until the theater went dark after the dance featuring Katya, Belinda, and Andre. But then the lights didn't come back on again for the curtain calls. The police found a device on the light-board that kept the lights out for a few minutes when everything went dark. Anyway, Katya said someone ran up to her in the dark and grabbed her. She felt the person tear the diamond pin from her costume and then she fainted."

At least, that's what she says, Nancy added to herself. She hated to think that the great Katya Alexandrovna might be involved in the theft. But Nancy had been fooled once before by someone who had faked a series of murder attempts against her own life, and she wasn't about to be fooled again. "What about the Raja diamond?" she continued. "How did it get to Chicago, and who do you think might have stolen it?"

James Ellsworth drew in a deep breath. "I'm afraid it's my fault CBT brought the diamond here. I was the one who contacted the Raja family and arranged to borrow the jewel for the new pas de trois." Then he added almost to himself, "It was great publicity, except that now it has backfired. With the new concert hall closed, the company's going to lose a lot of money. The old theater seats so many fewer than the new one."

"Well, it's pretty clear why someone would steal a million-dollar diamond," Nancy said. "But who had the opportunity to do it?"

"Colby Baxter thinks it was one of the dancers on the stage at the time. He's not letting either

Belinda or Andre dance. Of course, he insists that Katya continue to perform. He seems to think she's the only one around here who can do a decent pirouette." There was an edge to his voice as if he disliked both Colby and Katya.

"She's a very special dancer," Nancy commented.

"She's not as special as she once was," James said bluntly. "Personally, I think it's time to get some new and younger dancers out front. People like to see new talent, which means we sell more tickets, which is what a company is really about—tickets and money." He leaned toward Nancy, his eyes intent on her face.

Nancy studied his expression. She knew Colby Baxter and the dancers who made up CBT wouldn't agree with him. For them, dancing itself was the priority, not how much money each performance made.

The managing director frowned. "But what does Colby care about CBT's budget? Nothing! All he talks about is the artistry of dancing, and then he asks for another ten thousand dollars for new costumes. Let me tell you, Ms. Drew, this company would be in a complete mess without me."

Nancy had to smile. Actually, CBT's biggest problem right then was the missing Raja diamond pin. Since it had been James Ellsworth's idea to borrow it in the first place, some people might say

29

it was really *his* fault—even if he had had nothing to do with the robbery.

Nancy couldn't count him out as a suspect in the crime. He could have planned the whole theft and hired someone in the company to snatch it from Katya. Nancy had to look at all the possibilities.

"Well, the main thing right now is to catch the jewel thief," Nancy said. "And that's exactly what I intend to do."

"Good," James Ellsworth exclaimed. "You should look into Colby Baxter as a suspect."

"Right now, Mr. Ellsworth, *everyone* is a suspect," Nancy said meaningfully. "Is there anyone you can think of from outside the company who might have planned the robbery or stolen the gem?" she wanted to know.

The managing director pursed his lips. "Ana Lokhar was keeping a pretty careful eye on the jewel. She's the Raja family's representative here," he explained. "She was responsible for all the arrangements for the diamond. She's highly trusted by the family, but I think she's shrewd enough to have pulled off something like this."

I have the feeling that you are, too, Nancy added silently. But all she said was, "I'll check her out and Colby Baxter, too. Of course, I'll investigate everyone else, too."

"Fine."

"Tell me, Mr. Ellsworth, how are the police conducting the investigation?" Nancy asked.

"They're sure the diamond is still in the new concert hall. They searched everyone who was backstage last night, but no one had the gem, so they figure the thief hid it somewhere and will come back to retrieve it."

"Then they're concentrating on the new hall rather than this building?"

"Right."

"But what if the police are wrong and the thief managed to get the diamond past them? My best chance is to look for clues right here," said Nancy.

"Excellent. The police can keep things under control at the new theater and you can be responsible for what happens here. You've got your run of the building, Ms. Drew. Anyplace you want to search is all right with me." He glanced at his watch, and Nancy knew he was trying to tell her it was time to go. "Well, can I help you with anything else?"

"Not at the moment," Nancy said as she stood up to leave. "If I need to ask you any more questions, I'll let you know."

"Thanks again for investigating the case for us," the managing director said. He pushed himself out of his chair. "We can use all the help we can get." He laughed ruefully. "Come on, I'll walk you down to the lobby."

Together, Nancy and the older man walked out of the office and down the wide, carpeted stairway. But as they reached the bottom step, a well-built, red-haired man in sweat clothes came rushing up to them. From the expression on his face, Nancy could see that he was furious.

"Ellsworth, this whole scandal is your fault," the man yelled.

Nancy watched James Ellsworth's face grow tense. "Calm down, Baxter," he said. "Why don't you talk sense instead of getting hysterical."

"We're in the middle of a crisis and you tell me to calm down!" the artistic director continued yelling. "Don't you understand what kind of trouble this company is in because of your stupid publicity stunt?"

"Of course I understand. I'm the one who has to pay all the bills."

"Money," Colby Baxter scoffed. "That's all you can think of. What about the morale of the dancers? They're so depressed that half of them looked like zombies in class today."

"That's the least of our problems. I have the Chicago police on my back and the Raja family threatening to sue, so I can't worry about a few temperamental artists."

Colby's face turned an even darker shade of scarlet. "No, you never do worry about us, do you? As long as the ticket sales stay high, you don't give a hoot about this company! It's a good thing I'm around to maintain CBT's quality."

James flashed Colby a malicious grin. "Well, you won't be around for long. After this season, you're out of here. And I'm sure I won't be the only person to heave a huge sigh of relief!"

"You fool," Colby growled. "You couldn't care less what happens to CBT as long as the dollars flow in. You know, you're obsessed with money, Ellsworth. In fact, I bet you're the one behind the diamond's disappearance!

"Yeah," Colby continued as if the idea had just come to him. "You probably set up this whole publicity stunt just so you could get the Raja pin to Chicago to steal it!"

The managing director glared at the artistic director for a moment. Nancy could see James's rage gathering like a storm cloud. "How dare you accuse me!" he screamed. In the next instant James lunged at Colby, his hands reaching for the other man's neck.

Surprised by the sudden violence, Colby didn't have time to avoid the attack. James grasped his windpipe, his hands closing hard in a deadly squeeze.

Chapter

Four

COLBY GASPED FOR air as James's hands tightened around his throat. He was younger and, because of his daily dance workouts, much stronger than the other man. But he had been surprised and now had had most of the air knocked from his lungs. Without oxygen, he was ready to faint. He could not break free of the stranglehold. As James squeezed harder, Colby finally fell to his knees on the marble floor, almost unconscious.

"Stop!" Nancy cried. I've got to do something, she thought, before James kills him. Nancy grabbed hold of the older man's shoulders and shook them hard. "Let go of him," she cried. "You don't know what you're doing."

As the managing director turned toward Nancy in surprise, his grip on Colby loosened just a bit. That gave the artistic director the chance he needed. Thrusting his arms up with his last bit of energy, he knocked James's hands free and then lay back on the floor panting.

James was staring at Colby in amazement as if he couldn't believe what he had just attempted. "Good heavens," he exclaimed. "I never meant—" He broke off, too shocked to finish. "Colby," he finally got out, "are you hurt?"

Colby stood up, brushing off his sweatpants. The anger in his eyes still hadn't died. "You sure are strong for an old fool," he spat. Then he turned and strode out of the lobby.

James peeked at Nancy from the corner of his eyes and coughed weakly. "If—if you'll excuse me, Ms. Drew," he said, embarrassed, "we'll have to finish our conversation later." Then he walked up the stairs, his head bowed, his step unsure.

Nancy stood and watched him climb. It looked as if it were going to be a tough case. Tempers were flaring already, and she'd been investigating for only a few minutes!

The burst of violence was unsettling to Nancy, but she was glad she had been there to see it—*and* stop it. And after that incredible display of temper, both men were high on her suspect list.

Nancy thought about what had been said. Colby could be right—James could very well have planned to borrow the diamond just to steal it. After all, it was worth millions. And with his violent streak, she wouldn't put anything past him.

On the other hand, Colby had a reason for stealing the diamond—to blame its theft on James. It was quite clear that the managing director was behind the move not to rehire him for the next year. Colby could frame James and get back at the man who'd ruined his career with Chicago's top ballet company. And then he could sell the pin and never have to worry about money again.

Nancy reminded herself that all her theories were pure speculation. Either of the men could have planned the theft, as well as a score of other people. What she needed were hard facts.

Nancy went over to one of the lobby's couches and sat down to do some serious thinking. How did the thief get the diamond off the stage and past the police without being detected?

Nancy's guess was that the thief had concealed it somehow in a costume and smuggled it past the police. And if the thief had managed to get it off the stage, it was quite possible he'd gotten it out of the concert hall, too!

Okay, Nancy told herself, you've got a place to

start searching for clues. The costume storage room! One of the costumes worn last night has to have a secret place for hiding the diamond. Plus, I can check out Katya's costume to see if there are any secret hiding places there. And once I find the costume I'll know who it belongs to, and I'll have my thief.

Nancy twirled a strand of hair around one finger. Somehow, I have the feeling it's not going to be quite so easy!

For one thing, there would be over a hundred costumes to check. A couple for each of the dancers. Well, I obviously can't search all of them by myself. I'm going to need some help.

The image of one face flashed through Nancy's mind. Ned. But could she get him away from Belinda's dance class to go poke around a costume storage room with her? There was only one way to find out—ask him. Nancy stood up and, slinging the strap of her purse over her shoulder, she hurried up the lobby staircase in search of the dance studios.

A few minutes later Nancy was peeking around the door into a ballet class, motioning for Ned to come out and talk to her. She could see Belinda throw her a dirty look as Ned got up to leave the class.

"What's up?" Ned asked as he closed the door to the studio behind him. He looked a little nervous but also glad to see her. Funny, that was exactly how Nancy felt about being with him. "Even you couldn't have solved this case already," he added.

"No way," Nancy said. "In fact, I'm just going after my first clue and I need your help." Quickly she told Ned about wanting to search the costume storage room and why it was important.

"That's going to be harder than you think," Ned told her. "The police have put a padlock on the door to that room."

"But James said I could go anywhere to search," Nancy said.

"Anywhere but the storage room, I guess. But knowing you, Nancy, you'll find a way to get in there, anyway."

"Then you'll help me?" she asked, staring into his dark eyes.

"Hey, I'm the one who got you in on this case. I can't expect you to do all the dirty work yourself. Got any ideas about how to get past that padlock?"

Nancy patted her purse. "I came prepared— I've got my lock-picking kit with me."

Ned grinned. "Come on, Sherlock Holmes, we've got a whole lot of costumes to search."

For a moment their eyes met and all the old magic was back. Ned took hold of Nancy's elbow, and his touch made her knees go weak for a moment.

But as he steered her down a long, cream-colored corridor, Nancy did her best to squash the feeling. I have to get over him, she told herself. He's going out with Belinda now.

The CBT building was small, but it was dissected with many hallways branching off in all directions. And all these hallways on the second floor were painted the same cream color. It was incredibly difficult to tell one from another. Every office or studio Nancy and Ned passed looked just like the one before it. I'll have to learn my way around here, Nancy thought as she and Ned turned another corner. A person could get lost for days in these hallways.

"The costume storage room is right down here," Ned said, pointing ahead to still one more corridor, off which two other hallways ran.

"Ned, look!" Nancy cried as they turned the corner. "Someone is smashing the padlock on the costume room door."

The figure, dressed in black pants, a black sweatshirt, and a full black mask, looked up when Nancy shouted.

It took no more than two seconds for the unknown person to turn and slip quickly down a connecting hallway.

"Ned! Come on!" Nancy cried. She grabbed his arm and pulled him along as she ran after the black-clad figure.

The two detectives sped down the hall, turning the corner just in time to catch a glimpse of the mystery person slipping down yet another passageway. When Nancy and Ned turned down that passage they saw the figure hurry through a door that led to a stairwell.

Nancy and Ned lost sight of the intruder for just that instant. But it was one instant too long because when they opened the door and entered the stairwell themselves, the person was gone.

Chapter

Five

THERE WASN'T A sign of the figure in black moving in either direction on the staircase.

"Ned," Nancy cried, "we can't let that intruder get away. You head upstairs and I'll go down. If you don't find anything in fifteen minutes, meet me back at the costume storage room," she said as she took the steps leading down to the first floor two at a time.

"Be careful, Nancy," Ned said, calling back over his shoulder.

Once on the first floor, Nancy neither saw nor heard anything. She dashed quickly through the lobby and pushed the swinging doors open into

CBT's old theater. Nancy knew it well from the many times that she had seen the ballet company perform.

It was a beautiful but small theater with an oversize crystal chandelier and heavy purple curtains covering the stage. Row upon row of cushioned chairs stood before Nancy. And the intruder could be hiding behind any one of them—if the person was there at all.

There was nothing to do but start looking. Cautiously, Nancy made her way down the first aisle, checking each row for the figure in black. But the search took a long time. After five minutes, she had finished only half the theater, and she was beginning to worry that the person she was looking for had slipped away without her noticing.

"What are you doing here?" a voice rang out across the empty theater. "You're not supposed to be here."

Startled, Nancy turned to find a tall, blond woman walking toward her.

"I'm Mr. Ellsworth's assistant," the woman said sternly. "Who are you and why are you here?"

Great, Nancy thought. If the intruder's still here, this is the perfect chance to get out of here in a hurry. But there was nothing she could do about it. She had to deal with James Ellsworth's assistant right then.

As Nancy opened her mouth to explain who she

was, a second woman started down the aisle of the theater to join them. "I'm Nancy Drew," she said to the assistant. "I'm investigating the disappearance of the Raja diamond. Mr. Ellsworth gave me permission to search all the facilities of the building."

The assistant broke into a smile. "Oh, yes, he told me about you. My name's Liane." She extended her hand. "Sorry I interrupted you, but we've got to be extremely careful about security after this robbery."

The second woman had just joined them. "It seems rather late for that now!" she said. She sounded almost as if she were from England, but not quite. Nancy placed the accent immediately. The woman was from India.

Nancy turned her attention to her. The small, slim woman had dark skin, long shiny black hair, and large dark eyes.

Liane looked a little embarrassed. "Nancy, this is Ana Lokhar. She's representing the Raja family here in Chicago."

Ana eyed Nancy with a sour expression. "James told me about you, too. Actually, I'd expected someone older. I'm amazed that he'd trust a teenager!"

Nancy smiled slightly. She was used to people underestimating her abilities as a detective, and she'd always been able to prove them wrong.

She studied Ana Lokhar. The other woman was

wearing a pair of finely tailored black slacks, flat black shoes, and a pale flower-printed silk shirt.

Nancy looked more carefully at the woman before her. Could she have been the intruder? It would have been a simple matter of pulling off a black sweatshirt and mask. She had on the black slacks and shoes already. Could the shadowy figure and Ana Lokhar be one and the same? Nancy wished she had gotten a better look at the figure in black but she had seen it so fleetingly that she hadn't even been able to tell if it was a woman or a man.

The words that James Ellsworth had said about Ana Lokhar that morning came ringing back to Nancy. "She's shrewd enough to have pulled off something like this."

Certainly, it was possible. Ana had been in charge of all the plans on the Indian side for lending the diamond. She'd be in a perfect position to set up the theft. And since the Raja family trusted her so completely, the police wouldn't be likely to suspect her. The thing was, Nancy realized, that Ana would have had to have had an accomplice, someone to actually lift the pin from Katya. Nancy just couldn't imagine Ana sneaking onstage in the dark and grabbing the gem. In which case, Nancy would be looking for two thieves—the person who had planned the theft and the one who had carried it out. Ana could have recruited a helper, just as James or Colby could have, if either of them was responsible for the robbery.

Nancy flashed a tiny smile at Ana. "I'm sorry you don't have much confidence in me as a detective, Ms. Lokhar," she said. "But I know that in time I'll figure out who the thief is. In fact, I have a few suspects already."

Ana just stared at Nancy, her expression unchanged.

"Now please excuse me," Nancy finished. "I've got some clues to track down." She turned away from Ana and Liane and left the theater, knowing it would be useless to continue her search there. The thief would be long gone—if she hadn't already confronted her in the person of Ana Lokhar.

Once back on the second floor, Nancy couldn't remember exactly where the costume storage room was. She wandered down a few hallways, hoping she'd come across it or someone who could direct her to it. By the time she ran into someone to ask, she had already wasted precious minutes, and she hurried quickly down the hall the woman pointed out.

When Nancy got back to the room, Ned was nowhere in sight. Maybe he had better luck chasing the intruder than I did, she thought hopefully. Well, I guess I've just got to wait until he gets back here.

But then Nancy noticed something disturbing.

The padlock was no longer on its hasp. It was on the floor leaning against the wall, partially hidden by the door frame. That meant that someone had gotten inside since she and Ned had been there.

What if the intruder in black had come back and stolen the costume with the secret hiding place? That would blow any chance for an easy solution to the mystery.

Nancy couldn't wait for Ned any longer. She had to see what was in the room, to find out what kind of damage had been done. Cautiously, she pushed open the door, remaining in the hall and looking in. The hinges squeaked slightly as she stepped inside.

CBT's costume storage room was jammed. Tutus, leotards, loose-fitting street pants, ball gowns—just about anything possible to dance in—was carefully labeled and hung on three large rolling racks in the middle of the room. On the walls were shelves holding hats, headdresses, and props, all covered with plastic sheets.

It didn't seem to Nancy as though anyone had ransacked the room. That was lucky for CBT because if any of the costumes had been ruined, it could have killed their budget.

But the fact that the clothes looked all right didn't mean that the company hadn't lost something very important. If the intruder had snatched just one costume—the one which held the clue to the identity of the thief—she was in big trouble. It could mess up the investigation for weeks!

Nancy stared at the outfits, accessories, and the dozens of props stashed in the room. Searching for clues is going to be a gigantic job, she thought. I might as well get started. The sooner I begin, the sooner I'll find what I'm looking for. She took a few steps forward into the room and closed the door behind her.

As it swung shut, a silent figure, masked and dressed in black, was revealed standing behind the door. And that person was glaring at Nancy.

Nancy knew she had only a split second to act, and only time enough for a single thought. Obviously, I surprised the intruder in the middle of his or her own search, and now I'm in big trouble.

Nancy settled into a karate stance, ready to lash out at the figure at any moment if it should decide to attack her. She opened her mouth to scream.

But she never had a chance to get a sound out. The figure lunged—not for Nancy but for one of the heavy racks of costumes on wheels. With no time to jump out of the way, Nancy watched in horror as the crushing weight came hurtling toward her.

Chapter

Six

Nancy! Nancy, wake up! Please . . ." Somewhere through the fog that had overcome her, Nancy heard those words. All she could remember was the intruder in black pushing a rack of costumes down on her. Then she had slipped into blackness herself.

Now someone was calling her. With great effort, Nancy opened her eyes and peeked through. Ned was kneeling by her side, a look of frantic concern on his face. "Come on, Nancy. Please get up," he whispered as he reached out to stroke her hair.

Nancy couldn't help but smile. This was the old Ned—caring, attentive, loving.

"Oooh," Nancy groaned as she opened her eyes. Her body throbbed from where the costume rack had hit her.

"Nancy!" Ned exclaimed. "Thank goodness!" He threw his arms open and in another instant, Nancy found herself enfolded in his warm embrace. The hug lasted for one delicious moment. Then Ned pulled away gently.

And even though the hug had been brief, Nancy couldn't help but feel wonderful—despite her bruises! From the expression in his eyes, she knew Ned felt good, too. Unfortunately, she realized, he was now involved with someone else and couldn't let his feelings for Nancy show. Belinda was coming between them even in the deserted room.

"Are you all right?" Ned asked. He let the palm of his hand rest on Nancy's cheek.

"I think so," she replied. She stared into Ned's eyes for a moment. But then turned quickly away and got up, brushing dust off her jeans and sweater. "Hmmm," she said, glancing around the costume room, "it doesn't look like any damage was done to the costumes—except, of course, that they're all in a heap. But I hope nothing's destroyed or missing."

Ned laughed. "Nancy, you're the only girl in the world who'd be struck unconscious and then wake up with mystery on her mind. What happened, by the way?"

"I surprised a woman dressed in black in here, and she shoved that costume rack over on me."

"Woman?" Ned asked. "How do you know it wasn't a guy?"

"Well," Nancy answered. "I got a good look at her just before she pushed over those costumes. She was definitely female."

Ned got to his feet. "So what are we looking for? Let's get started."

Nancy smiled. "Thanks for offering to help, Ned. I appreciate it. Actually, I'm not sure exactly *what* we're searching for. Maybe something strange or damaged about a costume—if the intruder had to tear it up in order to get what she was after. Or it could be that we're looking for an item that's missing."

"Nancy, how are we going to find something that isn't here—especially when we don't know what it is that isn't here?"

Nancy laughed. "That's what being a detective is all about—solving impossible problems!" She and Ned stood the fallen rack up and began to rehang the costumes on it. Nancy searched that rack while Ned headed for one of the others.

The search progressed slowly, and even though neither she nor Ned found anything, Nancy loved every minute of it. Being with Ned, working on a case together—it felt just like the old days when they were a couple.

Nancy could tell Ned was having fun, too. He

really did love the excitement and adventure of detective work, even though he hated the amount of time Nancy devoted to it. He also hated the dangerous situations Nancy found herself in.

But to Nancy danger was just part of the game when she was investigating a mystery. The woman who had attacked her had certainly proven that.

"So who do you think rolled that rack of costumes on you?" Ned wanted to know as he carefully examined a pink satin costume.

"If I knew that, I'd probably have the mystery solved," Nancy said with a sigh. "But right now, I'm tending toward Ana Lokhar. I met her just now in the theater before I got knocked out. And, Ned, she was wearing black pants and shoes, just like our masked figure!"

Ned considered what Nancy had said. "That's an interesting possibility. With all her connections with the Raja family and CBT, she would have the opportunity to set up the heist."

"Right. And because the Rajas trust her so much, no one would be likely to suspect her! If she was ruthless enough to betray them, she'd stand to make millions with that jewel!" Nancy sat back on her heels. "I figure she came up to me in the theater to try to find out how much I knew and if I suspected her. When I left the theater, she didn't realize I planned to come back to the costume room, so she thought she could return herself to finish the job here while she had the chance. I got lost on my way back here and that would have given her just enough time to grab what she'd come for—"

"But you surprised her again and she had to knock you out," Ned finished.

Nancy frowned thoughtfully. "The problem is, it's just a theory. All the evidence is circumstantial. The intruder could have been any woman."

Ned shot Nancy a sympathetic look from across the costume room. "Don't worry. Whoever it is, she's not going to get away with it. Not with Nancy Drew after her!"

"Thanks, Ned," Nancy said with a smile as she pulled yet another outfit off the pile on the floor. "It sure feels good to have you rooting for me."

By the time Nancy had checked through the last of the costumes, she ached all over and was covered with fine dust. She hadn't found anything that looked even remotely like a clue—though she had gotten a few great ideas for evening dresses since CBT used fancy ball gowns in a number of their dances.

Nancy decided to look quickly around the room one last time. Under the rack, which she and Ned had stood up, she noticed one last costume lying on the floor. She picked up the white tulle gown with a pair of high heels slung over the same hanger. "Wow," she exclaimed. "It must be tough dancing in these."

But what was that she had uncovered lying on

the floor beneath the dress? Nancy reached down and picked up a small frayed piece of pink silk.

"Nancy," Ned asked, "what'd you find?"

Nancy examined the scrap of cloth intently. "It could be our first clue. The intruder might have left this here after she ripped apart some costume or . . ." Nancy knew she had seen fabric like that before. But where? Some skirt or blouse or pair of pointe shoes. She picked up her purse and said, "I'm not sure what this means—yet. But I intend to find out. I'm going to save it. Maybe one of the dancers will know where it came from." She opened her bag and dropped the piece of silk into it.

She dug around for her hairbrush. I must look like a total mess, she thought. And because Ned's been sneaking glances at me for the past hour, I think I should at least try to give Belinda some competition.

But before Nancy could find her brush, her hand closed around a folded piece of paper. Curious, she pulled it out and opened it. The typed message was short and to the point. Nancy read it out loud.

"'If you value your life, stay off the case.'"

53

Chapter

Seven

Nancy leaned back in her chair and watched the three figures on the TV screen whirl once again through the difficult steps that had ended so disastrously two days before. The dance company's video equipment was so good and the picture was so clear that Nancy hoped she would be able to see something that would give her a clue as to who could have stolen the pin.

Unfortunately Nancy was having a difficult time concentrating because the words of the note from the day before kept echoing through her head. The warning, on top of the attack in the costume room, truly frightened her because now she knew her attacker was someone who'd get violent before standing by and watching Nancy solve the mystery.

Maybe the intruder hadn't planned to hurt her—at least not yet. But she—and whoever she might be working with—had intended to slip her the threatening message because the note had been typed. That meant it had been written in advance. So she'd been waiting for the right moment to slip it to Nancy, and the encounter in the costume room had been perfect.

Nancy went over the list of suspects in her mind. Ana Lokhar was her prime suspect. But she hadn't counted out James Ellsworth or Colby Baxter yet. She knew neither man could have been the mysterious person in black. But either of them could have hired a woman from the company to help him steal the pin. So either of them could be responsible.

Leaving her troublesome thoughts for the moment, Nancy turned to her new boyfriend, Brad Eastman, who had come in with her from River Heights that morning to help on the case. "So what do you think?" She nodded toward the dancers on the tape. "Pretty fantastic, huh?"

"Sure is," Brad said, stretching his arm around Nancy's shoulder. He nodded his head slightly, his gray eyes intent on the screen. "CBT definitely has great video equipment. I guess they need it for their work."

"Brad, I meant the dancing, not the equipment!" Nancy said, holding back a groan.

"Oh, the dancing. That's nice, too."

Nancy sighed. Brad was a good guy, but sometimes he missed the point. "Do you see anything you think might help me figure out who stole the diamond?"

"I don't know, Nancy, it could have been anybody—maybe even someone in the audience!"

"How do you figure that?" Nancy asked. "They couldn't have sneaked on the stage—there are no stairs up to it from the auditorium."

"Maybe one of the dancers snatched it from Katya, then tossed it to somebody in the front row," Brad suggested.

Nancy rolled her eyes. "Not when the lights were off. The chances would be a million to one that the dancer would throw it to the right person. No one would plan a robbery this big and then do something like that. Besides, the orchestra pit is below the stage. He'd have to throw that diamond a long way to reach the first row of the audience."

"Oh," Brad said simply.

Nancy moaned. It was times like that that she really missed Ned and his clear thinking. As a partner on a case, Brad was the worst. He had no sense of how the criminal mind worked. And he was so overprotective of Nancy that he had practically begged her to quit when he had heard about the attack and the threatening note.

Of course, Nancy had refused to quit, so Brad had insisted on coming with her to make sure she'd be all right. He was on a break from law school, so he had time to join her. But it seemed to Nancy that he was getting in the way of the investigation, not helping. If anything dangerous did occur, she thought she'd have to protect Brad, not the other way around.

Ned used to worry about me when I was investigating a case, Nancy told herself, but at least he never doubted my abilities.

"Hey, Nancy, do you have a suspect yet?" Brad wanted to know.

"Sure," Nancy said. "In fact, I think I've got too many. Actually, finding suspects is never the hard part in a case. It's narrowing them down to the one person who's the criminal that's so tough," she explained.

"I see," Brad replied. Nancy knew he really didn't understand. He was probably the type who peeked at the last page of a mystery novel to find out who did it, instead of fitting the clues together himself. "Then who are your suspects?" Brad asked.

"Well, I'm keeping my eye on James Ellsworth, Colby Baxter, and Ana Lokhar because I think they'd have the best opportunities to plan the robbery—and the best motives, too. But someone had to do the actual stealing, and that someone was probably one of the dancers onstage. Which means Belinda, Andre, or Katya."

"Good," Brad said. "So now that you've got your suspect list, just give it to the police and let them handle it. Then you won't have to risk getting into danger yourself."

Nancy sighed again. "No, Brad, I can't do that." She was starting to wonder why she'd ever gotten involved with him.

"Well, don't get mad," Brad said with an easy smile. He let his hand slide down Nancy's arm and drew her close to him. Gently, he pulled her into a long, spine-tingling kiss.

Nancy shivered happily, giving Brad's muscular shoulders a squeeze. *That* was why she'd gotten involved with him. Brad Eastman was nothing compared to Ned, but there were certain times— and that was one of them—when none of that mattered. She let herself relax into his warm, thrilling kiss and forgot everything else.

Then the doorknob rattled, and she and Brad sprang apart. The door swung open, and a tall, stately blonde strode into the room. She was wearing an emerald green leotard and matching nylon warm-up pants, but even in her casual dance clothes, she looked glamorous. Her hair was pulled back into a perfect bun and the little makeup she wore accented her beautiful features.

"Katya Alexandrovna!" Nancy exclaimed as she came face to face with the great dancer. Nancy's heart beat a little faster.

Katya's face melted into a friendly smile. "That is my name," she said, her Russian accent still heavy in spite of many years of living in the United States.

"Oh, I've watched your performances for ages," Nancy said enthusiastically. "My ballet teacher always told me you were the best, and she was right!"

"How sweet. And who are you, dear?"

"I'm Nancy. Nancy Drew. And this is my friend, Brad Eastman."

"Oh, our resident private eye," the dancer said. "You know, most ballet groups have a company physical therapist or a company masseur. But CBT is the only company with its own detective."

"It's too bad the group needs one."

"Yes, that's true," Katya agreed. "The Raja diamond certainly has caused a lot of trouble. One little object like that shouldn't be able to make so many problems."

Nancy nodded. "I agree, but unfortunately, whoever stole it doesn't!"

Nancy watched the beautiful blond dancer carefully. It was incredible how charming she was—

not stuck up at all. Nancy instantly liked her and hoped they could become better acquainted.

But still, Nancy reminded herself, she couldn't count her out as a suspect. *Somebody* on that stage had to have snatched the diamond. And even though Nancy didn't like the thought, there was one chance in three that Katya could be involved.

Katya peered curiously at the video screen. "What is this you're looking at? A tape of the pas de trois?"

"Uh-huh," Nancy said. "I made it the night the diamond was stolen. I could have watched it at home, but the equipment here is so much better that I couldn't resist making use of it. Here comes the most important part!"

Katya, Nancy, and Brad watched as the three dancers on the screen began the final slow section of the dance. The two women rose onto their toes, their faces serene and calm. They looked perfect— not a hair out of place, not a wrinkle in their costumes, not a ribbon loose.

The theater thundered with applause as the lights went out. But just as Nancy remembered from watching the show on Sunday night, the clapping petered out after a few minutes and then Katya's scream pierced the theater. The stage brightened again, and Katya woke from her faint. And as they watched, Katya was helped offstage by the two younger dancers, her right foot was dragging slightly, and the ribbon of her toe shoe trailed behind her weak leg.

Nancy scrutinized the real Katya as she watched herself on the screen. She seemed displeased and a frown creased her features.

"What's the matter, Madame Alexandrovna. Don't you like what you see?" Nancy asked.

The dancer turned sharply. "No, no I don't. I don't look good in that video."

"Oh, the limp," Nancy said. "I was surprised to see that, too."

Katya caught her breath quickly and stared at Nancy for a moment, her expression hard. Then she said, "That's my weak ankle. It's been giving me more and more trouble."

Nancy smiled. "I thought so. And I'm sorry it's a problem for you. But it didn't seem to affect your dancing at all. You're still the greatest dancer CBT's got."

Katya's face seemed to soften. "It's kind of you to say so. Others are not always as generous. James Ellsworth, for instance. He wants younger ballerinas in the company, and even though I can dance circles around them, my ankle is all he sees." The ballerina shook her head. But then her face brightened. "Please, don't let me bother you with my problems. You have problems of your own—like this criminal who stole the diamond."

"I'm doing my best to find him," Nancy said with a smile.

"Well," Katya said, "I came up here only to get a videotape for Colby. I must hurry to class now." She pulled a tape from the CBT collection and walked to the door. But then she turned back to Nancy. "I wonder if you'd like to come watch the class. You seem to love ballet, so it might be fun for you."

Nancy caught her breath quickly and grinned. She was actually being invited to watch the CBT practice! "Oh," she cried happily, "I'd *love* to watch the class! Come on, Brad. Madame Alexandrovna's in a hurry." She grabbed her purse and took the tape of the pas de trois out of the recorder.

Katya laughed. "Your enthusiasm is wonderful."

Together, Katya, Nancy, and Brad left the video center and walked to one of the studios. The ballerina pushed the door open and practically knocked it into a young dancer who was on the floor doing sit-ups.

"Oh, excuse me," Katya exclaimed, stepping around the other woman. She bent down to talk to her. "Bridgit, did you find a pair of my pointe shoes in your bag? I think I may have dropped them in there by mistake a few days ago."

"Sorry, Katya," the younger ballerina groaned as she strained to do a few more sit-ups. "I didn't see them."

Katya stood up. "I'll have to make do with my new ones, then." She turned to Nancy to explain. "New shoes are very painful to break in. Well, I'm going to warm up a little before class. You two can sit in the chairs over in the corner. Enjoy yourselves!"

"I'm sure we will!" Nancy said happily.

She glanced around the brightly lit studio. Dancers were lying on the smooth wood floor, stretching, or standing at the practice barres that lined all four walls. A few freestanding barres were set up in the middle of the room, too. Mirrors covered two walls.

The dancers had left their bags in one corner so they wouldn't take up space on the dance floor. Nancy dropped her purse near these and turned toward the corner Katya had indicated. Maybe this would be just the kind of relaxation she needed to help her forget her troubles.

But just then Nancy glanced over and saw who was already seated in the same corner. Ned was there, so engrossed in a conversation with Belinda that he hadn't noticed Nancy come in. Belinda was sitting just a little too close to him for Nancy to feel comfortable. As usual, the dancer looked gorgeous. She was dressed in a pale blue unitard and her dark hair was pulled into a bun on the top of her head.

Nancy hadn't expected to see Belinda there

because she'd been pulled from the performances until the diamond was recovered. I guess, Nancy decided, she and Andre are still allowed to take company class. After all, they do have to stay in shape. She was glad, though, to see Andre there. She needed to question him about what had happened the night of the robbery. She'd make sure she got her chance right after class.

Nancy cast an unhappy glance at Ned and Belinda. Well, I suppose I'm going to have to face this sooner or later, Nancy told herself. As she and Brad approached the other couple, Belinda gave Ned a quick peck on the cheek and then stood up to join her class. As she passed Nancy, she gave her a haughty toss of her head.

Nancy and Brad pulled up chairs. Nancy linked her arm with Brad's when they were seated.

"Hi," Ned said. Then he whispered just loud enough for Nancy to hear, "Who's he?" Nancy hated herself for it, but she loved hearing the tinge of jealousy in his voice.

"That's Brad, my new boyfriend," she explained softly and introduced the two boys. Then she turned to watch the dancers stretching before class. It was amazing how hard they had to work! One woman casually picked up her foot and stretched her leg up around her ear. The dancer Katya had called Bridgit was still seated on the floor, her legs out to either side. She bent over and rested her chest on the floor between her legs in one easy movement. A man stood at one barre doing leg swings that were so high he almost brushed his face. And they're only warming up, Nancy reminded herself.

In a few minutes Colby Baxter walked into the studio, and the class musician hurried to the piano. The dancers stood up and took their places at the barre, the women's pointe shoes making a gentle thudding on the wooden floor.

"Let's begin," Colby said. "Two demi-pliés, two grands pliés, and a stretch forward in first, second, fourth, and fifth positions." He turned to the pianist. "Please take a moderate tempo."

The musician began a smooth, calming melody, and the dancers relaxed into the first exercise of the class. Nancy could see their muscles working as hard as any athlete's, but they made the whole workout look so effortless and graceful. It was beautiful to watch up close.

As the class progressed, the dancers began to sweat with their efforts. Yet they always remained serene.

Nancy sat enthralled. All the dancers were exceptional, but a few stood out as even more incredible than the others. Katya, of course, and though Nancy didn't like to admit it, Belinda. Andre Bernarde, the tall dancer with sandy-colored hair that curled down the back of his neck, was special, too. No wonder CBT had brought him from France to perform with the company. He had a beautiful presence. But did the mind of a criminal lurk inside that handsome body?

After about forty-five minutes of barre exercises, the first part of the class was finished. Then the dancers carried the barres out of the center of the room. Nancy watched Katya massage her left ankle gently. Poor Katya. Her ankle seemed to bother her all the time.

Colby continued the class with a more complicated routine in the center of the floor. As he demonstrated the slow, linked movements, Nancy realized why he'd been chosen as the artistic director of CBT. He was a wonderful dancer! It was sad that James was forcing him out of the company. They'd be losing a very special artist.

But Colby never finished showing the exercise. The studio door burst open, and Ana Lokhar breezed into the room, a man in a brown suit following on her heels. As he strode in behind her, he flashed a private investigator's license to anyone close enough to read it. James Ellsworth hurried in after them, also, a horrified expression on his face.

Uh-oh, Nancy thought. Something big's up, and I have a feeling it's not going to be pleasant.

Colby stopped in midstep and turned toward Ana, a disdainful expression on his face. "I'm teaching a class here. Why are you interrupting us?" His voice was as brittle as fine crystal.

"It's very simple," Ana explained, her expression every bit as disdainful as Colby's. "We are going to make a citizen's arrest. I'm having *her* put away." She pointed one finely manicured finger straight at Belinda.

Chapter

Eight

YOU CAN'T DO that!" Ned jumped out of his chair as the private detective walked toward Belinda to arrest her.

The class was in an uproar. Colby stood at the front of the room, his mouth open, his eyes round with surprise. James looked on uselessly, unable to move. And poor Belinda just stared as the detective approached her. She looked so frightened that Nancy couldn't help but feel sorry for her.

"Stop! You can't arrest her!" Ned cried again.

"No, you can't." In another instant Nancy was

on her feet beside Ned. Every eye in the room turned from the terrified Belinda to Nancy and Ned. "All right, what are the charges against Belinda Morrison," Nancy demanded.

"She stole the Raja diamond!" Ana cried, half-hysterical. "That priceless object belongs to the Rajas, and we want it back! Now!"

"Do you have any evidence?" Nancy demanded. "Without concrete evidence, it would be completely illegal to arrest her."

"I heard her talking about it on the telephone. She said she wanted to sell it, and then she would have all the money she needed."

Nancy turned to the dark-haired dancer. Belinda threw her a pleading look. "I was talking about my car. I swear. I never stole the diamond."

Nancy glanced at Ana. "It doesn't seem to me that you've got a very solid case. It's your word against hers, and it'll take more than that to convince a jury." She faced the man in the brown suit. "You ought to know better than to make an arrest on circumstantial evidence."

"She—she told me she had proof—" the man stammered, staring at the floor, embarrassed.

"Well, if you're not going to arrest this thief," Ana said, "I am getting out of here." She marched out of the studio, her head high. But Nancy knew that Ana must be feeling foolish. She had messed up, and she'd done it in front of a lot of people.

The detective followed her out. "Sorry for the interruption," he said. He shrugged feebly at Nancy as he left.

For a moment the room was completely quiet. Then, the entire company burst out into loud chatter. One handsome male dancer crossed over to Belinda and gave her hand a supportive squeeze. Colby stood glaring at James as if it were his fault Ana had interrupted the class.

Amazed at what had just happened, Nancy dropped back into her chair. She had gotten Belinda off the hook for the robbery—at least for the time being. But was she really innocent? She could have been lying about trying to sell her car, rather than the diamond. Nancy pursed her lips in concentration. Well, if Belinda *had* done it, Nancy would figure it out—and she'd get the evidence Ana had failed to find.

Nancy pushed her hair off her forehead. The other possibility was that Ana had stolen the gem and was trying to pin suspicion on Belinda.

It was also possible that the real thief was neither Belinda nor Ana. Nancy had four other good suspects, and any one of them could have been responsible.

It was awful having so few clues and so many suspects. But sooner or later, Nancy told herself, she'd come up with conclusive proof, something no one could ignore.

Ned moved over to Nancy, leaned down, and

whispered, "Thank you," in her ear. Her heart beat excitedly at his nearness. "You saved Belinda from all that and—and I don't know how to thank you."

Nancy's heart skipped a beat and sank. Every time Ned talked about Belinda, his face seemed to glow. But Nancy felt as if she had had a bucket of ice water dumped all over her.

Then Belinda walked over to them to join Ned. She smiled at Nancy with her usual sugar-sweet expression that Nancy hated. It was all so fake.

"Thanks for getting rid of Ana," Belinda said. "When Ned first said he wanted to ask you to help on this case, I wasn't sure it was a good idea. But he's so smart and clever that I should have known he'd be right."

Nancy stared at Belinda. What a faker! She glanced over at Ned, who was beaming. Nancy just didn't understand how he could be taken in by Belinda's act. "Well, I couldn't let them take you away *until* they have hard evidence, could I," she said innocently.

Colby clapped his hands together and silenced whatever Belinda would have said. "Okay," he said. "Let's get back to work. We were in the middle of an exercise!" He began to demonstrate the routine again, and the dancers quickly arranged themselves in loose lines in the center of the room.

Belinda glared at Nancy before hurrying to take

her place. Within a few minutes the company was working through a series of stretches and leg extensions. James Ellsworth pulled up a chair next to Brad's and joined the other three spectators.

If Nancy hadn't had so many things on her mind, the class would have been wonderful to watch. But she just couldn't concentrate. Her thoughts were whirling almost too quickly to sort out.

So she just let her mind wander as the whirling and leaping dancers passed before her eyes in a haze. Before she knew it, the workout was over and the company members were wandering over to pick up their dance bags.

Nancy stood up, easily stretching her own back. Quickly she shook her head and forced herself to look for Andre Bernarde. He was the only suspect she hadn't talked to yet, and she needed to get a sense of what he was like. The handsome dancer was standing at the barre in the far corner of the studio still doing a few final pliés. Good, Nancy thought, there's nobody near him so we'll be able to talk without being overheard too easily.

She turned to Brad and said she'd be right back. Then to Ned she said, "Bye. I guess I'll see you later."

"Sure," Ned replied. "That'd be nice."

Nancy smiled to herself. It seemed as though Ned really meant it. Then, slowly, she walked over to where Andre was working. She stopped near the handsome dancer, resting her hand on the smooth wooden surface of the barre. "Hello, Monsieur Bernarde," she said. "My name is Nancy Drew."

Andre turned to her in the middle of a plié. "Oh, the detective," he said, straightening his legs. His French accent was strong. "I knew you would come to interrogate me soon. You want to accuse me of stealing the diamond. Is that right?"

"I just want to ask you a few questions," Nancy replied.

But Andre acted as if he hadn't heard her. "Well, I didn't do it! I wasn't near Katya when the pin disappeared. I was on the other side of the stage!"

"Monsieur Bernarde, please, I'm not accusing you," Nancy said, trying to calm the dancer. "In fact, I need your help. You were onstage when the robbery happened. Did you see or hear anything strange?"

Suddenly Andre stopped, catching his breath. "No, Ms. Drew, I did not. And that's the odd thing, because I don't think anyone could have sneaked onto the stage so quietly that I wouldn't have heard him. It makes me suspect that one of the other dancers has to be involved—Belinda or Katya!"

Nancy studied Andre's face carefully. He acted desperate, and he was trying so hard—maybe just a little too hard—to deny that he was involved.

Was he on the level when he said he thought the thief must be one of the other dancers? Or was he just trying to throw suspicion off himself? Nancy didn't know enough about the man—or the case— to answer those questions yet.

"Can you remember anything else?" Nancy asked. "Anything that seemed even a little out of the ordinary?"

Andre shook his head hard. "I didn't see or hear a thing. I just stood in my proper place, waiting to take my curtain call. When the lights came back on, the diamond was gone. That is all I know."

Well, Nancy told herself, I guess that's all he's going to say about it. The dancer hadn't been much help, and it seemed as though he didn't intend to be, either.

But Nancy didn't let her annoyance show in the least. "If you remember anything later, please let me know."

"Yes, but I think I won't remember more," Andre replied.

As the dancer returned to his exercises, Nancy headed toward the pile of dancers' bags where she'd left her purse. Brad walked over and joined her, saying he was going out for a drink of water and that he'd meet her in the hall. Ned and Belinda had disappeared, as had James and Colby. Katya was sitting on the floor massaging her ankle. The room had pretty much emptied out, and only a few dancers were left practicing particularly difficult steps.

As Nancy grabbed the strap of her purse, she noticed that the zipper was open. I'm sure I didn't leave that undone, she thought. Then she noticed a white square of paper sticking out. With a feeling of foreboding, she pulled it out. Even before she opened it, she knew what it was—another threat letter. One of the company members must have slipped it into her purse before leaving the studio.

I should have paid much more attention to people while they were leaving, Nancy scolded herself. But I was too busy having that useless discussion with Andre, and so I missed a chance for a valuable clue! I've got to face it, I've been sloppy in my detective work.

Calmly, she unfolded the piece of paper.

We're both looking for the same object. But I am sure you won't find it. In fact, I challenge you to a race to see which of us can locate it first. The winner gets to keep the pin.
The Thief.

Nancy reread the note carefully, her heart beating excitedly. So the person who had stolen the Raja diamond didn't know where it was, either! How could that be possible?

It was her first break of the case. If the thief

didn't have the pin, there was no way it could have been smuggled out of the country. Nancy felt as though she'd gotten a reprieve.

She had no idea which of the dancers had hidden the letter in her bag. It could have been anyone. But who could have written it?

Nancy skimmed the letter once more. There was something about the way it was phrased that seemed familiar. Wait now, hadn't Ana just called the diamond, the object? Yes. She had said, "That priceless object belongs to the Rajas!" It was a small point, but it did link Ana with the note.

Somewhere in the back of her mind, Nancy remembered someone else using that same word to describe the missing pin. But who had it been? She couldn't quite remember. Was it Belinda? She couldn't be sure.

Nancy folded the letter carefully, suddenly feeling happy. Whoever the thief was had challenged her. And Nancy was never one to turn down a dare. In fact, the idea of competing with the unknown criminal made Nancy feel almost giddy.

I'm going to win this race for the diamond, Nancy promised herself. I'm going to win it if it's the last thing I ever do.

Chapter

Nine

"Brad, I have a very important assignment for you," Nancy said.

"You do?" Brad answered doubtfully.

"Uh-huh." Nancy pulled photocopies of the two threat letters out of her bag. "We need to check the type on these notes against that of the different typewriters around the CBT offices. If we can match the letters, we'll have a good lead to the thief."

"Great," Brad said enthusiastically.

"All you have to do is get samples of print from a few offices—especially James's and Colby's. It shouldn't be too hard. Meet me back here in the lobby in a half hour, okay?"

"Okay." Brad gave Nancy a kiss, then hurried up the broad lobby steps toward the main CBT offices. He seemed very intent on his mission.

He was so serious, in fact, that Nancy almost felt like laughing. By getting Brad busy doing something, she was free to investigate without being held back by him. Because of the challenge the thief had thrown at her the day before, Nancy was more determined than ever to find the pin.

Right then, Nancy's goal was to go to the dancers' lounge to talk to some of the dancers who weren't on her suspect list. It was possible that they'd seen something on the night of the robbery, something that they didn't even realize could be important. The relaxed atmosphere of the lounge should help people to talk freely.

Nancy opened the door to the lounge and found herself in a large, comfortable room with many couches lined up against the walls. About a dozen dancers were sitting around, reading, relaxing, or eating their lunches. Most of them looked pretty young—sixteen or seventeen.

"I've got to get some new pointe shoes," one of the dancers was saying. "A brand-new pair of mine disappeared yesterday."

"I lost some, too, along with my favorite unitard," her friend replied. "Someone's been stealing things lately."

Sure! Nancy said to herself. And the Raja diamond was the thief's major haul! She looked around for someone to quiz about the night of the robbery. In one corner she saw the girl Katya had called Bridgit in class the day before.

"Hi," Nancy said as she sat down next to her.

"Hi." She looked up from the magazine she was reading. "My name's Bridgit. You're Nancy Drew, the private detective, aren't you?"

"That's me," Nancy said.

"What an exciting thing to do!" Bridgit exclaimed. "It must be the greatest job."

Nancy couldn't help but laugh. "You know, watching all you dancers makes me think *you've* got the greatest jobs."

Bridgit nodded. "It is fun, but it's also exhausting. Sometimes I get so sore and tired I feel like quitting and hiding in bed for a month. But I suppose it's easier to see the good points of someone else's job."

"I guess so," Nancy agreed. "Right now, my investigation isn't going well, so *I'm* discouraged and feel like hiding in bed." Both girls laughed. "Actually, I was hoping you might be able to help me. Did you see anything the night the diamond disappeared? Anything strange or out of the ordinary?"

"Not really," Bridgit responded. "We were all busy getting ready for the big piece that was supposed to go on after the trio. Of course, we never got to perform it that night. So I'm sorry, but I didn't see anything."

Nancy was grateful, anyway. "That's too bad. I really need some clues. By the way, do you have a hunch about who stole the gem?"

Bridgit shook her head. "I think it could have been any one of the three dancers onstage. Andre keeps to himself a lot, so you never really know much about him. Katya will be retiring before too long, and I hear she's really worried about money. And Belinda is such a snob that she acts like the world owes her something. I wouldn't be at all surprised if she turned out to be the thief."

"Really?" Nancy asked. "You don't like her?"

"Nope. And neither does the rest of the company. She's a real flirt, too. She's always ogling my boyfriend when he picks me up after a concert."

Nancy frowned. I know what you mean, Bridgit, she thought.

"Anyway, I'm sorry I can't help you," the dancer finished.

"That's okay," Nancy told her. She glanced quickly at her watch. Why had she told Brad she'd meet him in half an hour? She wasn't going to have time to talk to anyone else. "Well, I've got to meet *my* boyfriend now," she said. "It's been fun talking to you, Bridgit. I'll see you around."

Nancy left the lounge and hurried down the long, empty corridors. She was eager to meet Brad and find out if the print from any of those typewriters matched the mysterious letters. Maybe that would finally provide the important clue she was searching for.

Because she got lost, Nancy accidentally found herself in front of the costume room. The padlock was still missing. Hadn't anyone replaced it after it had been smashed two days before? Or was the thief back again? Gently, Nancy leaned against the door and listened. She could hear voices coming from inside the room.

Being careful not to make a sound, she pushed the door slightly ajar and peered in through the crack.

Two people were pulling costumes off hangers and frantically inspecting them. Ana! Nancy recognized the petite woman's long dark hair. And the man with the wavy sandy hair was Andre!

"We *must* find the diamond," Ana said hysterically. "The pin has to be here in a costume! It's the only way it could have been smuggled out of the theater."

Andre threw aside a tutu glittering with rhinestones and began grabbing props off the shelves. Top hats, canes, even a plastic skull for the ballet of *Hamlet* flew onto the floor. He snatched up a blue felt bag and ripped it open.

All at once Andre stopped his wild searching and stared at something in his hands. He waved it excitedly in the air. "I've found it!" he cried. "Ana darling, look!"

Ana was at Andre's side in a flash. She snatched the sparkling pin from his hands and examined it greedily. Nancy's heart sank. They had the diamond. They had found it even before she had figured out they were the thieves.

Disgusted with herself, Nancy watched as Ana studied her prize. Nancy had no idea what to do. Should she rush in and confront the duo? No, Andre was incredibly strong and in fantastic shape; she wouldn't have a chance against the two of them. But if she ran to get help, Ana and Andre might be far away by the time she returned.

But as Nancy continued to peer through the slightly open door, she was shocked by what happened next.

Gently, Ana laid the jewel on the floor. Then slowly she raised her foot. With one sudden, violent movement, she brought the heel of her shoe down on the gem.

And the diamond shattered into a hundred pieces.

Chapter

Ten

ANA AND ANDRE stared silently at the shattered diamond. "Fool!" Ana hissed. "That was only a glass copy!"

Andre looked horrified. "I—I forgot that the company had a pin made of fake stones for the performances when we didn't have the real diamond to use."

"You forgot!" Ana said, raising her voice. "Well, you had better not forget any more important details." Nancy decided she wouldn't like to have Ana angry at her, and she couldn't help but feel a little sorry for Andre.

"Please, Ana sweetheart, don't scream," Andre

pleaded. "Someone will hear, and we're going to be in big trouble if they catch us in here."

"Until we recover the Raja diamond, I really don't care about anything," Ana replied, but Nancy noticed that she did lower her voice.

It seemed pretty clear to Nancy that Ana and Andre were dating, but she didn't have time then to wonder about their personal lives. She had to deal with their professional lives—which seemed to include big-time jewel heists.

Nancy tried to reason calmly. Ana and Andre hadn't actually said they had stolen the diamond. But it looked as though they had. But *why* would they be looking for the diamond if they had stolen it? Perhaps in the confusion of that night they had slipped it into a costume hanging on a rack and now couldn't remember which one. But why was Andre looking through the props? None of it really made sense, but Nancy still felt they had to be guilty.

She sighed. She needed help. Someone had to help her keep an eye on those two. Someone who could actually stop them if they tried to leave the theater.

James! Since Ana and Andre appeared to be the thieves, the managing director was cleared as a suspect for the moment. And he certainly wouldn't let the thieves get away because it would cost the ballet company so much money. But she had to notify him immediately.

Nancy took off to get Brad before heading for James's office. She ran down the back stairs to the lobby and pushed through the door with a bang. Brad was waiting. "Come on," she called. "I'm on to something important. We have to get moving," she said, running over to Brad and then turning to run up the stairs to the second floor.

"What's going on?" he asked, trailing behind her a couple of steps.

"I caught Ana and Andre destroying the costume storage room, looking for the diamond. It looks like they're the thieves. So now we've got to convince James to help us stop them—even without proof," she said over her shoulder.

"Uh, Nancy," Brad asked, stopping for a minute, "is this going to be dangerous?"

Nancy rolled her eyes and looked at him. "We're just going to talk to James. But we've got to do it now. Time is essential. Don't worry, we'll be fine."

They trotted down the second floor hallway to James's office. But when they got there, the managing director's secretary told them they'd just missed him. "I'm not sure where he went," the woman told them. "I think he might have gone to see Colby. Why don't you try his office?"

"Thanks!" Nancy called over her shoulder as she and Brad hurried to Colby's office next door.

No one was in the outer reception area, so when Nancy heard two hushed voices coming from

Colby's office, she went to the door to listen. Neither voice was James's. Nancy started to move away from the door, but then she heard something that made her stop.

"This company deserves every bit of bad publicity it gets." Colby had raised his voice and it drifted out clearly through the door.

"Come on, Nancy. You just said we needed to find James," Brad said.

"Ssh," Nancy told him sharply. "Listen." She motioned toward the office. "This conversation just might convince me that we've got another pair of suspects."

Nancy walked soundlessly back toward the office door so that she could hear every word. As Brad followed her, a floorboard creaked. "Be quiet," Nancy whispered. "We can't let them hear us."

"It's outrageous," Colby was saying. "James shouldn't be able to push you into retirement. But then he doesn't care about dance," he added bitterly. "All he's interested in is money. Money and publicity stunts!"

"Unfortunately, he has the power to do anything he wants with this company," the woman in Colby's office was saying. That Russian accent! Nancy recognized it immediately. It was Katya Alexandrovna! "If James Ellsworth wants to fire me, there's no one who can stop him. Because of

James, neither of us is going to have a job next year."

"Unless he gets blamed for the missing Raja diamond. The board of directors wouldn't keep him around after that."

Nancy caught her breath. Could Colby and Katya have stolen the pin to get revenge against James? If so, it was a brilliant plan. But just like Ana and Andre, they hadn't come right out and said they'd taken it. Either couple could still be guilty.

Oh, no, Nancy thought. Now I have two pairs of suspects—but no concrete proof against either of them. And even worse, no idea as to where the diamond could have been hidden.

Nancy could hear Katya's voice again. "The police are already—" But at that moment Brad coughed—very loudly. Katya's voice broke off in midsentence. "What was that?" she asked sharply.

"Come on, Brad," Nancy whispered urgently. "We've got to get out of here. Now!"

But before they could move a step, the door to Colby's office flew open. The artistic director and the ballerina stood glaring at them.

"Just what do you think you're doing here?" Colby yelled. With one smooth motion, he grabbed Brad with one hand and Nancy with the other.

87

Colby was extremely strong and his grip was quite painful. Nancy stared at him, horrified, as he squeezed her arm still tighter. What was he going to do to them? If he *was* the thief, he'd never let them go after what they'd heard. Somehow he'd have to get rid of them.

Chapter

Eleven

COLBY SHOOK NANCY and Brad furiously. Katya watched from inside his office, her face a mask, devoid of emotion.

"What are you doing here?" Colby repeated. Nancy could feel her arm being bruised under his grasp.

Nancy took a deep breath. This situation could be dangerous. Very dangerous. She'd have to handle it perfectly if she and Brad were going to get out of it unharmed. "Let go of us. You're hurting my arm," Nancy told Colby plainly.

Katya calmly walked over to the artistic director

and laid a hand on his shoulder. "Relax," she said. "Don't get so excited. They're only a couple of kids playing detective."

Colby stared at the ballerina for a moment, then dropped Nancy's and Brad's arms. "You're right, Katya." He glared at Nancy. "You shouldn't listen in on other people's conversations, young woman. Didn't your parents ever teach you any manners?"

Nancy didn't know how to answer Colby because he was now treating her like a kid and not like a detective at all.

"Look," Nancy began, shifting her gaze from Colby to Katya and back, "I'm just trying to find out who stole that pin."

"Well, we certainly didn't take it," Katya said. "Why don't you concentrate on your suspects, not us?"

I'm not so sure you didn't, Nancy answered silently. But she couldn't say that out loud—until she had proof. So, angry as she was at Colby, she had to accept it for the moment. She'd bide her time and keep her eye on the pair.

"You won't catch me eavesdropping again," Nancy answered simply. No, they wouldn't catch her. But that didn't mean she wasn't going to do it anymore. It just meant she was going to be smarter.

"All right, now get out of here, you two," Colby said brusquely. "And if I find you here again, I'm going to call your parents."

Nancy glanced once more at Katya. As always, she seemed completely in control—not at all as if she'd just been overheard having a suspicious conversation. Did that mean the things she and Colby had been saying to each other really weren't important? Or did it mean the ballerina was just a very good actress?

Whatever the truth was, she and Brad had to get out of there. Nancy grabbed his hand and pulled him from the room.

As soon as they were in the hallway, Brad turned to Nancy. "That was terrifying," he burst out.

Nancy smiled, holding back a giggle. "That was nothing! I've been in worse trouble than that—a lot worse." She thought back to a mystery she had solved in Florida recently. She had almost been killed then, but it hadn't made her give up the investigation. Not at all.

"Well, that's not anything to be proud of," Brad said, his voice angry. "I think you should quit this case. It's much too dangerous."

Nancy shook her head. "I'm sorry, Brad, but I'm sticking with it until I figure out who stole the diamond and where it is."

Brad smiled and gave in grudgingly. "Okay. But you'd better do it fast, Nancy. I don't think I can take much more of this."

Brad was right. She *did* have to solve the mystery quickly—but not because of any personal danger to herself. If she didn't find the diamond soon, the thieves would. And that would put a speedy—and disastrous—end to the case.

"Belinda is going to be dancing the lead in *Giselle* next week!" Bridgit exclaimed.

It was early Thursday morning, the fourth day of her investigation, and Nancy had stopped in the dancers' lounge to have a cup of tea before going to work. The samples of typewriter print Brad had gotten the day before hadn't matched that on the notes from the thief. So Nancy was back in the lounge, talking to the dancers.

Luckily, Brad had decided to stay home that day, which meant it would be a lot easier for her to work.

"Well, that shouldn't come as a surprise," the girl sitting next to Bridgit replied. "She's been buttering James up for the past few days."

"Yeah. As usual, James went over Colby's head and got Belinda back to work. She did 'something' to help him, and he's paying her back by helping her."

Nancy put down her cup of tea and turned to Bridgit. "What did she do?"

"Who knows," Bridgit answered. "I asked her about it, but she told me to mind my own business."

"It could have been anything," the second dancer explained. "James always has a million fund-raising ideas that he tries to get us involved in—you know, benefit shows, parties, anything that will bring in the big bucks. Usually we say no because he doesn't pay us. But I guess he's paying Belinda, though."

"He sure is, and not just with favors. I saw him hand her a wad of bills you wouldn't believe," Bridgit cut in.

Nancy picked up her tea again. So Belinda had helped James with a well-paying job. But instead of bragging about it, she had clammed up to Bridgit. How strange. Obviously, it was no ordinary piece of work. Could it be, just maybe, a diamond heist?

At that point it wouldn't surprise Nancy at all. She had Ana and Andre as a pair of suspects, and Colby and Katya as another, and now she'd discovered a link between her last two suspects.

"Do you know any way I could find out what Belinda did for James?" Nancy asked the two dancers.

"I don't know. Maybe you could ask her boyfriend. You know that tall, cute guy she's been hanging around with? He seems really nice, and he might know more about what Belinda's been up to than we do."

Ned! Of course. But Nancy was worried about how he'd react to an accusation against his new girlfriend. She knew the conversation could get more than a little tense. But if I want to make sure

Belinda's innocent, I've got to do it. I have to check out all the possibilities.

Nancy said goodbye to the two girls, and abandoning her tea, she hurried out of the dancers' lounge.

Nancy thought she'd have to call him at home, but he was already outside the women's dressing room, waiting for Belinda. Things must be serious for him to be there so early in the day.

"Ned," Nancy called from down the hall. "How've you been?"

"Okay." Ned threw her a warm smile. "How about you?"

"Oh, I'm all right, too," Nancy said. "But I need to talk to you."

"Sure," Ned said easily. "What's up?"

Nancy stepped away from the dressing room door. "Well, I heard Belinda's going to be performing again."

"That's right." Ned's smile widened. "Isn't it great news?"

Nancy coughed uncomfortably. "Uh, yes, but I hear James pulled a few strings to get her back on the stage. And since they're both still on my suspect list, I wondered if you knew why he was doing it for her."

With a sinking heart, Nancy watched Ned's smile fade. "Nancy, what are you implying? That Belinda stole the Raja diamond for James, and he paid her back by putting her onstage again?"

"Uh, I guess I am," Nancy answered lamely.

"I can't believe this," Ned exclaimed. "You're jealous. And you're letting your jealousy interfere with your sleuthing!"

"But, Ned, I'm just trying to—"

Ned wouldn't let her finish. "What you're trying to do is force the blame on Belinda. It's ridiculous, and I'm not going to stand around and listen to any more of this!" Turning his back, he stormed off.

Nancy stared after him—his words had really stung her. Great, she thought. Now I've really blown it.

But Ned stopped in his tracks a moment later as a figure dressed completely in black appeared at the end of the hallway. Its face was hidden by a black mask. The shadowy figure stood still for just one long moment, then quickly disappeared down a side corridor.

"Nancy," Ned cried, "did you see—"

"I sure did," Nancy broke in. She dashed up to him and, grabbing his hand, took off down the hall after the person in black.

As Nancy and Ned turned the corner, they caught just a glimpse of the mystery figure whipping around the next one. It's almost as if the thief is baiting us, Nancy thought. But we've got to keep going. Right now, it's our only sure lead to the thieves!

The figure in black dashed down hallway after

hallway until Nancy and Ned weren't sure where they were. But they were gaining on it, inch by inch. Suddenly Nancy poured on the speed. With a burst of superhigh energy, she threw her purse to Ned and dashed forward, determined to end the chase.

In a desperate attempt to escape, the figure raced toward the freight elevator, threw the door open, and jumped into the dark interior.

But before the door could close all the way, Nancy was at the elevator herself. Grabbing the metal door with her left hand, Nancy shoved it open as she stepped out with one foot—into empty space. There was no elevator—only a thirty-foot fall and instant death.

Chapter

Twelve

NANCY WAS LEANING into the empty shaft, balanced precariously with one foot dangling in space. She clung desperately with her left hand to the door. But because so much of her weight was forward and pulling her down, her hand started to slip. Do something! her mind screamed. Do something or the next few moments are going to be your last!

Frantically, Nancy reached out with her right hand and grabbed the metal door frame—just as her other foot slid out from under her and she began to fall. With both arms stretched spread-eagle, Nancy could feel the cold metal in both her hands slide against her palms as she began her death plunge. There was nothing on the door or frame to stop her hands from slipping.

The sides of her hands cracked when they struck a hard ledge. The floor! Her hands were now resting against the hallway floor, still clutching the cold metal of the door and frame. The floor was the only thing saving her from certain death at the bottom of the elevator shaft!

Nancy was dangling, but at least she wasn't falling anymore.

She looked back and up into Ned's terrified face.

"Nancy," Ned cried frantically, "hold on! Please, hold on!"

"Uhhh," Nancy groaned. "I intend to, believe me." Her arm muscles were beginning to ache, but they were far from giving out.

Ned lay down on his stomach, then grabbed both Nancy's wrists. Cautiously, Nancy wrapped her hands around Ned's wrists. Inch by inch, Ned hoisted Nancy's body higher out of the dark chute. His every muscle strained.

Finally, Nancy's thighs were clear of the floor, and in one swift move she swung her legs up onto the floor, then rolled quickly away from the empty shaft.

Nancy just lay on the floor panting, her eyes closed.

"Are—are you okay?" Ned asked.

Nancy opened her eyes and pushed herself up to a sitting position. "Yes," she said softly. "I am a little shook up, though. If it hadn't been for you . . ." She left the rest of the sentence unfinished.

"I know," Ned answered. "It's too horrible to think about."

Just then they heard what sounded like a mad scramble up the inside of the elevator shaft. They ran to the ledge and looked up to see a rope dangling down from the floor above. The figure in black must have climbed up the rope to the third floor. When the person jumped into the dark shaft the rope was hanging there ready to be grabbed. He or she must have been hanging just above Nancy and watching her as she struggled to save herself.

"Ned, I've got to solve this case soon," Nancy burst out. "The thieves threatened me before, but now they've actually made an attempt on my life!"

"I'm all for getting them out of the way fast," Ned said with passion.

"The thing is," Nancy continued, "I don't even have a hunch about which of my three pairs of suspects actually did it."

Ned frowned. "Well, just eliminate Belinda and her so-called partner, James, from your list and that will cut your possibilities by a third."

Nancy frowned back. "I'd do that, Ned, *if* I were sure they weren't the thieves!"

Ned stared at Nancy silently for a moment, his dark eyes meeting her blue ones. "Please, let's not go through this again. Not now."

Nancy sighed. Ned was right. There was no reason to talk about it. They would both just say the same things again. Nancy felt the anger draining from her, leaving only warm feelings for Ned.

She reached over and gave his arm a friendly squeeze. "Well, whatever happens with this case, I'm glad you were here, Ned, to help me. Nobody could have handled that situation as calmly as you did!"

"Don't worry, Nancy. I'll always be there for you when you're in trouble. I promise."

Nancy hesitated for a moment. Right then she really did feel as if she were in trouble—big trouble—over this case. She needed to get it all clear in her head. Maybe reviewing all the possibilities slowly and out loud would straighten her thoughts out. Could she ask Ned for his help? It was worth a try.

"Um, Ned, there is one little thing you could do to help me. I'd like to talk the whole case through with you—that is, if you're not busy right now."

Ned smiled. "Sounds like fun."

"Good," Nancy said. "But I *am* going to have to talk about Belinda a little. Will you *promise* not to get mad at me?"

Ned smiled. "I think so—just this once at least," he said teasingly. "But we'd better not talk

100

here. Come on. I saw an open room not far from here."

Ned led the way to a large room down a corridor by itself. Tentatively, he pushed the door open and stepped into the company costume shop. After she walked in, Nancy removed a pin cushion from a stool, pulled it up close to a table, and sat down. Ned pulled another stool close to hers, and they both rested their elbows on the smooth cutting surface.

"Okay," Ned said. "First of all, what are your clues?"

"Well, the first one's got to be somewhere in that videotape I made. I know something has to be on it that will tell me who took the pin, but I just can't see it."

"What else have you got?"

"That piece of torn silk that we found in the costume room—I checked costumes, shoes, everything, to see if it might match. The silk could have come from either a costume or slippers that the intruder ripped up." Nancy pushed a strand of hair out of her eyes. "Plus," she continued, "dance clothes and slippers have been disappearing around this place. Katya was looking for a pair of her pointe shoes, and a few of the others have lost shoes."

"Yeah," Ned added. "Belinda said a few of her things got stolen, too."

"And then there are the threat letters. They

called the diamond an 'object,' and so did Ana. I'm sure another person used that same word, but I can't remember who!"

"Those clues are all good for starters," Ned said. "Now, how about describing your suspects to me."

"Well, there are Ana and Andre. Their motive would be plain greed. She's a good bet because she made all the arrangements to bring the diamond here for the Raja family. And since they trust her so much, people wouldn't suspect her too easily. Another thing that makes me wonder about her is the fact that she was wearing black shoes and pants when I met her—just like the masked intruder, who was a woman. Also she was very aloof when we spoke."

"And as you just told me, she used the word *object* when she was talking about the diamond," Ned added.

"Right. And if Ana is involved with Andre, she would have a perfect accomplice to help her set up the elevator trap. He's strong and athletic and could have easily pulled himself up the rope."

"Who's your next pair of suspects?"

"Belinda and James." Nancy glanced at Ned, but he seemed okay. "Their motive would have been greed, too. Belinda was holding Katya when the lights went on after the robbery and that makes her a prime suspect. *And* she barely says a word to me, which makes me think she may have something to hide.

"James would have had just as good a chance to set up the heist as Ana—he made all the arrangements on the American side. And I hear that both James and Belinda have a lot of money these days. I don't think James would be strong enough to pull himself up the rope, but Belinda would."

"Sounds like circumstantial evidence to me," Ned muttered under his breath.

"Katya and Colby are my last pair of suspects," Nancy hurried on. "Their motive would have been the money plus getting back at James for not renewing their contracts at the end of this season. Katya acted as if the thief had hurt her during the robbery, but she could have been faking that. Colby's definitely strong enough to have been the masked intruder—and Katya is no weakling herself. Either one of them could have climbed the rope."

"I don't think the solution to the mystery is that far away," Ned said encouragingly. "You have quite a bit of information."

"But not quite enough to figure the whole thing out. I'm sure everything I need to know is here, but I'm just not putting it all together right."

"You will," Ned said. "I'm sure you will."

"But can I do it before the thieves find the diamond? Somewhere in all those clues is the key to the pin's hiding place. I've *got* to figure it out."

Nancy glanced around the costume shop. Twelve almost completed lavender leotards were neatly hung on hooks. Obviously, they were new costumes for the corps dancers. She also spotted two short, pink silk camisole dresses and a man's black pants and shirt.

"Ned," Nancy asked curiously, "do you recognize those costumes over there?" She pointed to the pink dresses and the man's outfit.

"Aren't those the costumes from Belinda, Katya, and Andre's trio?" Ned asked.

"They are!" Nancy answered.

She stood up and walked casually over to the clothing rack. She fingered one silky skirt. The hanger had Belinda's name pinned to it, and a pair of pale pink pointe shoes were slung around it.

Katya's costume was identical, except for the tear on the bodice where the jewel had been attached. Nancy looked around for her pointe shoes, but they were missing. There was a beat-up old pair of slippers in their place. Nancy knew Katya hadn't worn *those* onstage.

Andre's black outfit was made of soft cotton, and a pair of black jazz shoes was hung with it.

"Well," Nancy commented, "if the diamond was hidden in any of these, the police definitely would have found it. The fabric is so thin that there can't be many places to hide it. But I wonder what happened to Katya's shoes? Maybe they were ruined during the search. They—"

But Nancy didn't get a chance to finish her sentence because she was interrupted by one short clicking sound at the front door. A key had been turned in the lock on the outside of the door.

Ned and Nancy rushed to the door. She twisted the knob with all her strength and gave a hard shove. The door didn't budge. She rattled the knob and pushed again. Finally she slammed her shoulder against the door even though she knew it was no use. They were locked in!

A spine-chilling laugh rang out from the other side of the door. It was a mocking laugh, evil and menacing. Then there was only the faint sound of footsteps as Nancy and Ned's jailer slipped away.

Ned angrily turned and kicked at the door a couple of times. "What do you think he's going to do to us locked up in here? Nancy, what's the point of making us prisoners in the costume shop?"

"He's just showing us that we're completely at his mercy—he's in charge. Anything can happen now, and you can bet we won't be shown any pity!"

Chapter

Thirteen

Well, what do you suggest we do?" Ned finally asked. "We can't bang on the door. No one will hear us. We could be locked in here for hours."

"No way," Nancy told him. "I always come prepared. Now where did I leave my purse?"

Ned spotted it and walked back to the table to scoop it up. He brought it back to her. "I suppose you've got a hacksaw in here to cut us out of this place?" he asked, joking.

"Nope. Something a lot easier to carry around than that," she answered. Taking her purse from

Ned, she rummaged through it until she found her lock-picking kit.

"You know, Nancy," Ned said, "it's a good thing you're honest. No one would have a chance against you if you were a thief."

"Just call me Fast Fingers Drew," Nancy wise-cracked. She slipped an extremely thin-bladed tool resembling an ice pick into the keyhole and twisted for a few seconds until it caught. "Here, hold this pick in place while I jimmy the rest of the lock."

Ned grasped the tool steadily as Nancy worked two other picks, one with each hand. After a couple of minutes of intensive concentration, she could feel the pins of the lock moving. A moment later it sprang open. Nancy gave the doorknob a twist, and she and Ned were free.

"I should have been an escape artist," Nancy said, laughing.

"Actually, I think you're doing just fine as a detective," Ned told her.

"Not on this case I'm not. I'm not at all close to solving it."

"Nancy, we just went all over this. You've got a lot of information. More than you think. And I know that pretty soon the answers will fall into place." Wrapping an arm around her shoulders, he gave her a warm squeeze.

Nancy was savoring the sweet rush of emotions

that flooded over her when she glanced up to meet Ned's warm, dark eyes to see if he was experiencing the same feelings.

After returning her gaze for a couple of seconds, Ned looked away and slowly and gently removed his arm. Nancy was instantly jolted out of her reminiscing.

Still not daring to look at Nancy, Ned took a deep breath and asked quietly, "So, what's next? About the mystery, I mean."

"I knew what you meant, Ned," Nancy said just as quietly.

Now he looked embarrassed. He hadn't meant to let Nancy see how deeply he still cared for her.

Nancy finally broke the still lingering spell by speaking.

"Well," she said, expelling the breath she had been holding unconsciously, "Bridgit said the dancers were too busy getting ready for their number to notice anything the night of the robbery. But I can't help feeling that they know more than they think they do. I mean, they always seem to know everything that goes on in the company."

"It's true," Ned agreed. "Belinda says everybody knows everyone else's business."

"They sure found out fast enough about her getting reinstated and dancing the lead in *Giselle*. I'm almost positive they could provide the single clue that would clear up this case. They just don't know what they saw and know."

"You could be right."

"I'm going to check out the dancers' lounge again," Nancy said thoughtfully. "It couldn't hurt."

"Sounds good," Ned said and finally found the courage to meet Nancy's gaze.

The two stared at each other silently until finally Ned took a deep breath and shrugged. "Okay, Nancy, I won't keep you from your sleuthing anymore. Good luck." He flashed her a tight little smile before he walked out of the room and started down the hallway.

Sadly, Nancy watched him go. Her heart quickened for a second when he turned back, but he just raised his hand in a casual wave and continued on. He'd been her best friend as well as her boyfriend for so long, but now there were walls between them. Walls that just wouldn't come down. Trying to forget her sadness, Nancy hurried down the corridor toward the dancers' lounge.

When she got there, she found Katya Alexandrovna carefully applying ice to her left ankle. "Hi," Nancy said. Despite the unpleasant scene she and Brad had had with the star ballerina and Colby, Nancy still respected her as a dancer. And Katya *had* told Colby to let them go, after all. There was no reason for Nancy to be unfriendly.

"Hello," the dancer returned. She nodded toward the ice bag. "The ankle's acting up again. Cold is the best thing for it."

Nancy nodded. "I know a lot of athletes use ice for muscle problems, too."

Across the room a few of the younger female dancers were sitting around in their practice clothes. They were talking about which guys in the company were the cutest. Right then they looked like any group of teenagers getting together for an after-school gossip session. It was funny to think that they were also professional dancers.

Nancy said goodbye to Katya and crossed the room to sit on a couch near the younger dancers. It felt wonderful to be able to relax without having to worry about the masked intruder. She silently eavesdropped, listening for any clues the ballerinas might drop without realizing what they knew.

"I think Robert Sierra is pretty neat looking," one of the girls was saying. "And his leaps are thrilling."

"Give it up, Lindsay," another girl said. "He's much too old for you."

Lindsay groaned. "Who isn't in this company? They hire all of us young, but the guys are a lot older."

"I know. It's such a drag," one of the others agreed. She picked up her bag and began searching through it. "I'm hungry. Anybody want a carrot stick?"

"Sure," said a girl with bright red hair and a face full of freckles.

"I'll take one, too," another piped up.

Nancy smiled to herself. *That* was the difference between these girls and her own friends. No junk food here. Many of the dancers watched every calorie they ate.

The girl pulled out a bag of cut carrots, but she kept looking through her things. "Hey, where are my pointe shoes?" she said, annoyed. "I'm sure I put two pairs in this morning, but now there's only one."

"Oh, no, not again. I've lost two pairs already this week. Someone's been stealing shoes," the redhead exclaimed.

"But why?" the first girl wondered. "I mean, whoever took them couldn't possibly wear all those shoes. Besides, no one would want to use someone else's pointe shoes. There's no way they'd be able to dance in them."

"Hey, pass me one of those carrots," said the girl who liked Robert Sierra.

Her friend handed her the bag, and pretty soon the group was busy talking about the guys in the company again.

But Nancy had stopped listening. Stolen pointe shoes. She'd been hearing a lot about stolen shoes since she'd gotten to CBT. She remembered how Katya had asked Bridgit if she'd found a pair of her shoes. And the first time she had come to the dancers' lounge, some of the ballerinas had been saying they, too, had lost shoes. Katya's missing shoes in the costume shop that day were probably just another example of the same thing.

Nancy remembered the torn piece of silk she and Ned had discovered in the costume storage room. She hadn't been sure if it was part of a costume or a small bit of a pointe shoe. Now she was convinced it was from a dance slipper. A slipper that the black-clad intruder had ripped apart in his wild search for the diamond.

Slowly Nancy began to develop a theory. The diamond must have been hidden in a pair of pointe shoes. That was how the thief had smuggled the diamond past the police and out of the new theater. If the jewel were wrapped up in lamb's wool—which the dancers used to pad the toes of their pointe shoes—and stuffed in a slipper, it would be the perfect way to safeguard the stolen pin and smuggle it past the police.

But when the costume people carried the costumes back to the old theater, the thief must have lost track of the shoe with the diamond. And no wonder. There'd been costumes, personal possessions, and makeup to move. And that included pointe shoes belonging to thirty women!

Quickly Nancy calculated. If each girl owned five or six pairs, that would mean three or four hundred individual shoes to pack up and bring back to the old theater! It wasn't at all surprising that the thieves had lost track of the right one!

Okay! Nancy told herself excitedly. All I have to do is find that shoe and I've got the diamond!

But Nancy knew it wouldn't be at all simple. After all, the thieves had been searching among the shoes for four days already. They had a very big head start, but, she consoled herself, they hadn't found it yet. She still had a chance. It would be a huge undertaking, but after the thieves had tried to kill her that morning, she was more determined than ever!

Her theory didn't tell her *who* had stolen the gem, but at least she could recover the stolen property.

Nancy quickly checked to see if Katya was still there. There were some important things she wanted to ask the group of dancers, and it would definitely not be a good idea to do it in front of one of her prime suspects. But the older ballerina had already left.

Nancy leaned in toward the girls. "Excuse me, I couldn't help hearing what you said about your pointe shoes disappearing lately. Maybe I can help you out." And if I'm lucky, she added, you'll be able to help *me* out.

"Oh, you're the detective who's investigating the diamond robbery," the redhead said. "Sure, it would be great if you could find our shoes for us. It's very painful breaking in new shoes."

"Well, the first thing I need to do is take a look at some of your shoes."

"Okay," the girl said. She pulled two pairs out of her bag and handed them to Nancy.

"What's so special about these?" Nancy wanted to know. "I mean, why wouldn't any other dancer want to wear them?"

"Pointe shoes aren't all the same," the dancer explained. She turned one slipper over and pointed to a tiny letter engraved in the middle of the hard leather sole. "See, that letter stands for a particular shoemaker. Each one sews the slippers slightly differently. T's shoes feel great to me, but Sondra here gets horrible blisters from them," she said nodding at one of the other girls.

"Well, it's possible that the ballet shoe thief is really looking for a pair of slippers she lost earlier," Nancy suggested. "So if I help find those slippers, maybe the thief will leave your shoes alone. Now, where might the person who's looking for her shoes have put all of yours?"

The red-haired dancer shrugged. "If we knew that, we'd go get them. But I guess you could try the dressing rooms, the studios, anyplace and every place. Sorry I can't be more helpful, but I just don't know."

"Well, in that case I'd better get started looking right away." Nancy grabbed her purse and hurried out of the lounge.

"Good luck," she heard one of the dancers call after her.

* * *

By the end of the day Nancy's feet ached. She had been all over the CBT building searching for shoes, but she hadn't found anything.

And somehow, while she was looking, she had mislaid her purse. She was incredibly annoyed at herself. She shouldn't have been so careless. Her money, her car keys, her driver's license—everything was in that bag. If she didn't find it, she was going to have to leave her car in Chicago all night and try to catch a ride home with Ned. Nancy sighed. This definitely hadn't turned out to be a very good day. Nancy dragged her feet down the steps to the lobby.

All of a sudden she stopped short. Sitting in the middle of a couch in the middle of the lobby was her purse! "I *know* I didn't leave that down here," she exclaimed out loud. Picking up her pace, she hurried to the couch.

Nancy grabbed up her purse and cautiously opened it. There, as she had guessed, was another square of folded white paper—another note from the thieves! Slowly she opened it and read.

Either you've developed a foot fetish, Nancy Drew, or you've finally figured out where the pin is hidden. But stay on your toes because I'm looking for the diamond, also. Too much is at stake for me to let you get it before I do. So be warned, I'll do anything to keep you from ruining my plans. Anything!

Chapter

Fourteen

Nancy pressed her lips passionately against Brad's. He wrapped one arm around her waist and pulled her closer to him on the Drews' couch.

"Mmm," he murmured. "This is absolutely the perfect way to spend a Thursday night."

Nancy responded with yet another kiss. "When I was little, I used to hate the times Hannah was out and my dad worked late at the office. But now that I'm older, I realize that it does have a few advantages."

Brad leaned back against the sofa, and Nancy rested her head comfortably on his shoulder. "So," he asked, "what movie did you rent?"

Nancy coughed. "Uh, I thought we'd watch a video I taped off the TV." She knew Brad wasn't going to like her choice of entertainment.

"Sure, anything you want," Brad said, stroking Nancy's hair lovingly. "I guess it really doesn't matter what we put on the VCR." He laid another kiss on the top of Nancy's head.

Nancy squeezed Brad's hand, then stood up and popped the cassette into the VCR. She pushed the play button and the TV screen lit up with a view of the stage. Soon three dancers—Katya, Belinda, and Andre—came whirling onstage, moving through the carefully choreographed steps of CBT's now notorious pas de trois.

"Nancy!" Brad yelled, totally frustrated. "You're doing more detective work! I thought we were going to have the evening to ourselves—no father, no interruptions, and most of all, *no mystery!* Don't you ever take a night off?"

Nancy shrugged sheepishly. "Sorry, Brad. I guess until this case is over, you're just going to have to learn to appreciate ballet."

Brad crossed his arms over his chest. "I don't *want* to. And I don't want to help investigate this crazy mystery, either. Can't we have just one night alone?"

Nancy dropped back onto the couch. "Not yet, Brad, but soon, I promise. Just as soon as I've solved it."

"All I wanted was a nice easygoing relationship

and what do I get? A live version of an Agatha Christie novel."

But Nancy was already so engrossed in the moving figures on the screen that she barely even heard him. The clue that would solve the mystery had to be here. And this time she'd catch it!

Nancy checked every tiny detail, her eyes jumping from the dancers to the background to the Raja diamond sparkling on Katya's bodice, searching for the smallest, most easy-to-miss clue. But there was nothing out of place. Everything seemed to be perfect.

Finally the lights went out at the end of the dance, and when they came back on, one ear-splitting scream and a few moments later, the Raja diamond was gone. Katya woke up from her faint, then slowly limped toward the wings with Belinda and Andre supporting her on either side. The picture made by the exiting star ballerina was quite beautiful and poignant. Her head was bowed, and the ribbon of her pointe shoe trailed behind her.

"Hey, wait a minute," Nancy cried suddenly. "I think I've found my clue!" Jumping up, she pushed the rewind button on the VCR, then quickly pushed the play button once again. She studied the three dancers for an instant before stopping the machine. "I was right!" she exclaimed. "Brad, look!"

Brad sat forward, a confused expression on his face. "What, Nancy? I don't see anything wrong."

"That's exactly the point," Nancy said excitedly. "Here"—and she poked the play button once again—"at the beginning of the dance, everything is all right. Now look at this." She pushed the fast forward button and the machine sped forward to the last shot of Katya leaving the stage. "Katya's right ballet shoe! It's untied here! But it wasn't before."

"So?" Brad asked. "What's the big deal?"

"Think—pointe shoes don't just untie themselves. Someone did it on purpose. And the only person who could have done it was Katya!" She scrutinized the dancer. "And there's something else that's most important. Katya's limping on her *right* side. But today in the dancers' lounge, she was putting ice on her *left* ankle, and she said *that* was her weak ankle.

"Brad, that's it! While the lights were out, Katya untied her shoe and put the diamond in it. But then, of course, she couldn't help but limp. She covered it up by claiming it was her bad ankle, and no one ever caught on that it was the wrong leg!"

"But I still don't see how she got the diamond past the police," Brad said. "I mean, they searched all the costumes, right?"

"Yes, but the dancers got out of those costumes

119

in their dressing rooms, first. Even with a police-woman watching her, it wouldn't have been hard for Katya to exchange her pointe shoes with the diamond in them for an old pair. It would have taken only a second. And then she could just walk out of the theater with the diamond in her shoes and the shoes in her bag—no suspicion. The only thing I don't understand is how she then lost the shoes."

"It's a good theory," Brad said. "I think it actually could have worked!" A gleam of enthusiasm began to show in his gray eyes.

"And it explains why the shoes I found attached to Katya's costume in the costume shop were old ones, obviously not the clean new ones she wore during the performance. So Katya has to be the one who stole the diamond. And Colby's in on the heist with her. He probably planned the whole thing to get back at James for letting him go at the end of this season and then convinced Katya to help him pull it off."

"Nancy!" Brad cried. "I think you've done it! You've solved the mystery!" He threw his arms around her and gave her a huge hug. "Finally, we're going to be able to get back to normal around here!"

Nancy pushed Brad back gently. "Not quite yet. I've still got a lot of work to do. I won't be finished until I find the diamond and have Colby and Katya arrested."

"But now you can go to the police and let them handle the rest of the case, right?"

Nancy shook her head. "Sorry. It's still my responsibility. Besides, laying my hands on that pin is going to be the most satisfying part of the mystery! I definitely won't give up that moment."

Brad groaned. "You have got to be kidding."

Nancy stared at Brad, her gaze holding his. "No, Brad. I've never been more serious in my life. I'm going to find that diamond. Nothing's going to stop me now. Nothing!"

Nancy had been so excited Thursday night that she had barely slept at all. She had just kept going over her theory again and again. Even after she had been through the whole scenario half a dozen times, she couldn't find any flaw in her thinking.

At the theater the next morning she was determined to get the evidence she needed to put Colby and Katya away—and she was determined to get the diamond. That meant keeping a close eye on the two thieves.

Tentatively, she knocked on the door of the studio where Colby was rehearsing Katya for a new solo piece. "Who is it?" came Colby's voice from inside the studio.

Nancy opened the door and stuck her head into the room. "Hi," she said. "I heard you two were working together in here. If it wouldn't bother you, I'd really love to watch. I've never had the chance to see anyone with your talent rehearse before."

Colby hesitated, then turned to Katya. The tall, blond dancer broke into a smile. "Certainly, dear," she said, her Russian accent heavy.

Colby looked puzzled. "Are you sure?" he asked.

"Of course," the dancer replied. "Come in and have a seat." She motioned to a chair in front of the mirrors.

Nancy stepped inside and shut the door firmly behind her. "Thanks," she said. She had the feeling Colby and Katya knew she was stalking them, but for some reason they didn't seem very worried. Or at least Katya didn't. Why? Nancy wondered. Could they have found the shoe with the missing diamond in it?

She was pretty sure they hadn't because the warning note she had gotten the day before said they were still looking. It wasn't likely that they'd found it since then. At least she hoped they hadn't.

Colby walked over to the tape deck and pushed the play button. Lush symphonic music poured out of the speakers. "Okay," he said to Katya, "let's take it from the beginning of the second section."

Katya marked a few steps, her movements very small, until the music came to the right spot. Suddenly she broke into full, smooth dancing. The result was breathtaking. To Nancy, it looked flawless.

But after a few moments, Colby clapped his hands to stop the dancer. "The extension in arabesque should begin on the count of five, not four. Let's try it again." He rewound the tape, and Katya began a second time.

The two artists ran through the dance over and over, making minor corrections, arguing over the rhythm of the steps and searching for that tiny extra bit of stretch that would make the dance perfect. To Nancy, it was a fascinating process.

She could see that both Colby and Katya pushed themselves very hard. They weren't satisfied with the piece until they'd been over it countless times. They were incredibly dedicated and talented. It was unthinkable that James had decided not to rehire the two of them. Nancy could almost sympathize with them for stealing the diamond in order to get back at James Ellsworth.

Almost. But not quite. All Nancy had to remember was their attempting to kill her in the empty elevator shaft.

"What do you think, Katya?" Colby finally asked after an hour and a half of nonstop rehearsing. "Should we call it quits for the day?"

"No! I think the piece could use quite a bit more work. Let's continue."

"Okay," Colby replied. He rewound the tape once more, and Katya began all over again.

Nancy listened to the short conversation intently. All through the rehearsal Colby and Katya had been having little exchanges like that. Colby would turn to Katya and ask her opinion. Then, whatever Katya decided, they would do, just as when Nancy had asked to watch the rehearsal. Colby hadn't decided until he checked with Katya first.

And she remembered how Katya had persuaded Colby to let her and Brad go when they'd been caught eavesdropping. It was becoming very clear to Nancy that Katya really knew how to control the artistic director.

Also, it was becoming increasingly difficult to imagine Colby as the brains behind the diamond theft. As it was hard to imagine Katya being manipulated by him. Katya's personality was much stronger than Colby's.

And finally something Katya had said kept coming back to Nancy. "One little object like that shouldn't be able to make so many problems." She had said that the first day they had met in the video room. Finally it dawned on Nancy that *she* was the one who had used the word *object* to describe the gem. And that meant she had written the threatening letters, not Colby.

Nancy felt like shouting. Colby didn't plan the robbery, Katya did!

Nancy watched the beautiful dancer extend her leg perfectly. Of course, Nancy told herself, I should have seen it long ago. Colby's so devoted to Katya that he'd do anything for her—and he probably has. Like luring me into the elevator shaft!

I've got to finish this case once and for all, Nancy thought urgently. Katya's private dressing room—I've got to search there. Suddenly Nancy felt as if she couldn't wait one more second. I have to search that room—now. And since Katya and Colby are going to be rehearsing for another hour, I've got the time to do it without being caught!

The next time the dancers stopped for a moment, Nancy spoke up. "Uh, thanks for letting me watch. I've really learned a lot! But I've got some stuff to do myself, so I think I'll be going. Thanks again."

"See you later," Katya called as Nancy hurried out of the studio.

It didn't take Nancy more than a few minutes to find Katya's dressing room and jimmy the lock. She stepped in and closed the door quietly behind her. Seven or eight pairs of pointe shoes lay under the vanity table and Nancy went for those first. But, as she already knew, there was nothing inside any of them.

Nancy turned the slippers over and inspected the numbers and letter on the hard leather bottoms. "Size five, double A, made by X," Nancy said softly to herself. "That information might come in very handy later."

She carefully replaced the shoes, then slid open the vanity drawer. Stage makeup, false eyelashes for performances, hair clips, baby oil for removing cosmetics—the drawer was a jumble of small items. Nancy reached way into the back of the drawer. If there was anything hidden in the vanity, it would be there. But she found nothing.

Suddenly the door of the dressing room flew open with a startling bang.

"I had a feeling I'd find you here," Katya cried. "That's why we cut our rehearsal short. And I've caught you with your hand in my vanity table. Nancy Drew, what right do you have to be here?"

Nancy snatched her hand from the drawer and turned to face her accuser. Her heart was pounding, but she did her best to sound calm. "When I began this case, I got clearance from James Ellsworth to search any place for the Raja diamond. Right now, that means here!"

To Nancy's surprise, Katya didn't get furious. Instead, she laughed. "You sound like Ana when she tried to get poor Belinda arrested. Who me, a jewel robber? What a crazy idea. Why would a famous, successful dancer want to risk ruining her career for a diamond? I've got plenty of money— and plenty of jewels of my own."

"For revenge!" Nancy countered. "Revenge

against James Ellsworth for not rehiring you for next season."

"No, dear, I am retiring. It has nothing to do with James. Because my ankle is weaker now, I feel that the time is right. James made sure everyone in the press knew."

Nancy sucked in her breath. Katya definitely knew how to cover her tracks. How was she ever going to convince people that her suspicions about the dancer were true? The answer was, she couldn't, not without the diamond itself.

Katya was staring at Nancy.

"These thieves are dangerous," she said in a monotone, her eyes vacant and staring, her jaw set in a taut line. "If you mess up their plans again, it could be the last mistake of your life. And, Nancy, we wouldn't want anything horrible to happen to you, would we?"

Chapter
Fifteen

A RE MY LASHES on straight, Ellen?" Bridgit turned to one of the other dancers and fluttered her false eyelashes at her.

Ellen giggled. "Yeah, but you need a little more mascara on the left one," she said teasingly.

Bridgit made a face. "What are you trying to do, get me onstage looking like an idiot?"

"No one can tell from the audience," Ellen countered. "Besides, people never watch us corps dancers, anyway, only the principal ballerinas." She peered into the mirror herself, applying an extra few drops of rouge.

Nancy shook her head and joined in the conversation. "You're wrong about that. I always check out the corps. I'll bet I'm not the only one, either."

"Okay," Ellen said, "I'll take your word for it."

Nancy smiled. It was great fun watching the corps ballerinas preparing for that Friday night's performance. They smoothed their hair into perfect buns; a dab of Vaseline kept any stray hairs in place. A few were already dressed in their tutus, while others were still warming up in their sweat clothes.

Actually, it was hard to believe these girls were about to dance in front of hundreds of people. They joked and laughed as if they were getting ready for a high school play.

The evening was going to be exciting, Nancy was sure. CBT was premiering a new version of the classic ballet *Giselle,* with Belinda dancing the lead role. And even though Nancy still didn't like her very much, she couldn't deny that Belinda was a magical dancer. She wouldn't have missed the show for anything—except finding the Raja diamond.

And, if she were lucky, being backstage with the dancers might just give her some idea about where those missing shoes were.

Nancy knew she should go and join Brad, who was sitting alone, waiting for her in the wings. He was stuck watching yet another ballet, but he'd said he'd come that night to keep her company.

And now she'd deserted him. But she felt it was important to listen and ask questions in the dressing room. At least they'd be backstage together during the show. She needed him, also, in case Katya and Colby made another attempt to intimidate her into silence.

Of course, Brad hadn't been much help in the past. But if *he* weren't able to help, there was always Ned—he'd be backstage, too. And Nancy knew she could count on him if anything got out of hand.

"Hey, Marlene, could you zip me into my costume?" Ellen called across the dressing room to one of the other dancers.

"Sure," Marlene said. She stood up and walked toward her friend in her still untied shoes. She tugged on Ellen's zipper, then tied a satin bow at the top of the costume. Sitting down again, Marlene began to lace up her slippers.

"Did you find the pointe shoes I left near your locker?" Ellen asked her friend. "I saw they were your size, so I figured they belonged to you. I guess they must have fallen into my bag by accident."

"Oh, was that you who put them there?" Marlene wanted to know. "Thanks for returning them, but they weren't mine. They were the right size but the wrong shoemaker. They were heavy, too. Must have been a crummy manufacturer."

Nancy couldn't help but join the conversation.

"Uh, where did you say you put those shoes?" she asked Marlene seriously. She couldn't hide the urgency in her voice because she was remembering a few days earlier when Katya had asked Bridgit if she had found some shoes that she might have accidentally put into her dance bag. She could have mistaken Ellen's bag for Bridgit's. Maybe these were the shoes that Katya was looking for. The shoes that Nancy was looking for herself! The shoes with the Raja diamond.

Marlene shrugged. "I just left them lying around the corps dressing room. I figured the dancer they belonged to would find them."

"You said they were the same size as yours," Nancy remarked. "What was that?"

"Five, double A. I can't remember the maker, though."

Nancy gasped. The same size as Katya's! It couldn't be just a coincidence. They had to be the ones in which the prima ballerina had hidden the Raja diamond.

Nancy bit her lip thoughtfully. Perhaps it really had been an accident that Katya's shoes had gotten mixed up in someone else's bag. Then again, Katya probably put them there on purpose in case the police did happen to search her bag as she left the theater. That way, there wouldn't be any chance of her getting caught with the pin. What she hadn't counted on was Ellen finding them first and trying to return them.

But the shoes! Where were they? Nancy shuddered slightly at the thought of them lying around the dressing room. Anyone could have picked them up.

Hardly daring to think about the horrible possibilities, Nancy turned to Marlene and Ellen. "Uh, what do you think happened to those slippers?" she asked them.

"Beats me," Ellen answered. "The person who owned them might have found them. Or they could have been thrown out."

Nancy's eyes widened. The idea that the diamond was now at the bottom of some garbage heap outside of Chicago was just too awful.

"Or maybe someone tossed them in the lost and found," Marlene piped up.

The lost and found! "And where's that?" Nancy asked quickly.

"On the second floor. It's a huge cardboard box sitting in the hallway near the costume room," Marlene replied.

"Thanks," Nancy exclaimed as she hurried from the dressing room. In an instant she was halfway out the door. She ran as fast as she could through the backstage area to the back stairs. Not stopping for an instant, she ran up them.

This is it! I've almost got the shoes—and the Raja diamond! She poured on an extra burst of speed.

Nancy shoved the stairwell door open and went flying down the hall toward the costume room. The cardboard box wasn't hard to find. Leaning over, Nancy rummaged through the old leotards and T-shirts, sweaters and sweatpants. There was a pair of beat-up old jazz dance shoes and— Nancy's hands closed on some pointe shoes!

With the blood pounding in her ears, she gently pulled them out of the heap of lost items. They were well worn and the satin was dirty. Her heart racing, Nancy checked the size. . . . A tiny number six was etched into the hard leather sole.

Oh, no, they weren't the size fives she was looking for. Just to make sure there hadn't been yet another mix-up, she reached into the toe of each shoe. Nothing.

Nancy could almost taste her disappointment. There had to be another pair somewhere in that heap of old clothing. She dropped the size sixes on the floor beside the lost and found.

Bending over farther, she began churning up the items from the bottom of the box. The next pair of shoes she found were a size four, which she placed on the floor next to the sixes.

Suddenly Nancy heard a faint sound. She held her breath, listening intently and trying not to make any noise. Her ears strained to hear the next sound.

For a moment there was only silence. But wait,

there it was again! The faint echo of footsteps moving down the hallway toward her. The sound was soft and utterly terrifying!

Colby and Katya must have seen her speeding up there and then one of them must have sneaked up to follow her.

Nancy's first instinct was to get up and run! But what if the shoes really were there, and she just hadn't found them yet? She couldn't leave them for Katya or Colby.

Frantically, she pulled the lost and found box over. Tights and leg warmers and old unitards came tumbling out all over the polished floor. And there! Nancy could see them! A pair of gleaming, new, pink satin pointe shoes tucked together in a neat bundle.

Nancy glanced over her shoulder. At the end of the hallway, a masked, black-clad figure had just appeared from around the corner. He had the broad shoulders of a man, so Nancy knew it had to be Colby. Even though she knew who was behind it, the dark mask still frightened her. Wait! What was that? Something was in his hand, catching light on its shiny surface. A knife!

Nancy knew she was out of time. Not bothering to check the size of the pointe shoes, she grabbed them and took off down the hallway. She ran quickly, but Colby wasn't far behind. And he had the stamina of a professional dancer.

With no one in sight, Nancy was more than a little frightened. She accelerated until she felt as if her heart would burst from the effort.

And still Colby didn't slow down—he was gaining on her. The sound of his footsteps pursuing her echoed through the hallway.

Chapter

Sixteen

Nancy clutched the million-dollar ballet slippers to her chest as she continued her mad dash to the stairs. If only she could make it down to the theater . . . Brad and Ned would be there—it would be safe.

There! Just ahead! The door to the back stairwell. It would lead her directly backstage, straight to Brad and Ned and anyone else in the wings who could help her. She was pushing herself to the limit; her legs were growing heavy; she desperately needed oxygen. Just two more steps. One . . . She'd made it!

She slammed her hand into the door and sent it

flying open. Then she started down the steps, taking them two at a time. The theater's backstage was only a few feet away, but Colby was in the stairway, too, and Nancy could almost feel his knife seeking her out.

She catapulted down the remaining steps, pushing off against the banister and throwing herself into the wings. Out of the corner of her eye, Nancy could see that the performance had just started.

Dancers were crowded everywhere, waiting for their entrances and going over steps in their minds. They were too involved in preparing to go on to realize what was happening to Nancy. She nearly knocked a fragile blonde over as she barreled into the wings, Colby right behind her.

"Hey!" the ballerina exclaimed.

But Nancy just kept running. Colby wasn't going to let those shoes slip away from him. Of that, Nancy was sure. She had to get far away from him—and fast!

Where were Brad and Ned? She was in no position to go looking for them. If she stopped for only a moment, Colby would be upon her instantly with his knife. One jab and that would be the end of her. She'd be badly hurt or—or dead! Colby would grab the shoes and, if he were lucky, get out of the theater with them while everyone was still confused.

Dead ahead Nancy spotted a ladder, bolted to

the floor. It led up to the metal grille above the stage. Maybe she could escape Colby that way!

Still grasping the precious ballet slippers, Nancy headed for the rickety old ladder. Suddenly she realized that she'd be alone on the catwalk far above the stage—with only Colby, who would pursue her even up there.

Nancy quickly decided that it would be better to cross to the other side of the stage to look for Brad and Ned. Flattening herself against the back wall, Nancy slid sideways between the backdrop and the back wall. The space was barely six inches wide.

Colby was following right beside her.

"Colby," she whispered. "What are you trying to do? You'll never get away with this with all these people around."

But Colby only gave a muffled laugh. "I'm willing to bet that I can," he hissed.

"You haven't caught me yet," Nancy cried. She kept sidestepping, desperate to get away from Colby, until she was free of the curtain.

At last she spotted Ned on the far side. He was staring at her and at her black-clad pursuer with terror in his eyes. "Nancy," he shouted.

Katya Alexandrovna, standing next to Ned, looked almost as terrified as he did—but for very different reasons. Everyone backstage turned to see what was going on. Obviously, the noise was just too much to ignore.

It doesn't matter now, Nancy told herself.

The chase was taking every ounce of her strength. But her legs ate up the space to Ned.

"Nancy, hurry!" Ned cried urgently.

"Ned, move left," Nancy shouted back. A plan was forming in her head, but first she had to get Ned away from Katya Alexandrovna. She couldn't risk letting the ballet dancer intercept the shoes. "Go out for a long pass. And whatever you do, don't drop the ball!"

Ned wasn't sure what she was up to, but he didn't hesitate a moment to run left and back as far as he could. Nancy lifted her arm, the ballet shoes clutched tightly in her hand. By then, Colby was just two steps behind her, and Nancy knew she didn't have a moment left to spare. With a snap of her wrist, she sent the shoes spiraling toward Ned. A split second later, Colby's hand closed around her arm.

But it was too late. The shoes were already sailing through the air toward Ned in a perfect arc. Fantastic, Nancy thought. Guess all that practice tossing a football around with Ned came in handy! Without that pass, Colby would have gotten the shoes.

Colby dropped Nancy's arm and dashed toward Ned at breakneck speed. He had no hope of getting away now, but still he was dead set on capturing the shoes. Brad started after him, but Colby was too far ahead for him to stop.

Nancy had new problems of her own now.

Katya Alexandrovna was coming at her—and there was murder in her eyes.

Nancy sank into her well-practiced karate stance. She just got to catch a glimpse of Ned snatching the ballet slippers out of the air before Katya lunged for her.

Nancy was ready for Katya's kick, but Katya's movements were so different from the ones she had practiced against in karate class. Katya's leg came into a perfect passé position, her pointed toe just touching the knee of her other leg. Then in a flash she struck out with her foot. Nancy lashed out at her with her fist, but Katya had already danced out of reach. Then the ballerina came at her with a whirling, kicking turn. If Nancy hadn't been quick enough to scoot away, she would have been hit with the old one-two—first Katya's powerful right leg, then her sturdy left.

This is incredible, Nancy thought, Katya is using ballet to fight me! But I can't let it break my concentration. I have to take Katya out!

The next time Katya danced toward her, Nancy held her ground. Now the ballerina let loose with a few regular well-aimed and strong punches. Nancy had to work hard to avoid them.

Katya swung at Nancy with her left fist. Nancy ducked and spun out of arm's reach. The ballerina kept coming at her, though, hitting out again and again. Each time Nancy danced away, Katya attacked once more. But Nancy was biding her time. Katya was a surprisingly good fighter, but she'd make a mistake at some point. Nancy just had to keep out of her way until then!

Then Nancy saw her chance. Katya's timing on the last punch was just a little off. When the dancer's right fist came at her, she was ready. At the crucial moment, Nancy grabbed Katya's forearm and twisted it. She gave Katya's shoulder a shove and she fell to the floor. Nancy pounced on her and held her in a practically unbreakable karate hold. Nancy felt great. That move worked every time.

"Let me go!" Katya sputtered.

But Nancy kept a firm grip. A group of dancers stood around them, not sure which of the two they should help—the young detective or Katya.

Still holding Katya tight, Nancy looked across to where Ned and Colby were now fighting. They were moving dangerously close to the open stage and with each punch, it seemed as if they might crash into the set and onstage in full view of the whole audience.

Colby's mask had come off, and a group of corps dancers were staring in surprise and confusion. Colby swung a punch, but Ned caught his arm in midair, giving him a shove backward. Colby sailed onto the stage, a new and surprising addition to *Giselle*.

Ned followed him onto the stage, kicking out with his foot.

A piece of scenery teetered unsteadily as Ned's foot brushed against it. The canvas and wooden flat came tumbling down right on top of Ned and Colby!

The dancers stood and stared. The orchestra had long since stopped playing. Belinda looked like the fairy-tale princess who had just kissed a frog, but had found out that this time he wasn't going to turn into a prince. Finally the curtain puller closed the stage drapes.

Beneath the canvas flat no one moved. By craning her neck Nancy could just see one of Ned's hands sticking out.

"Ned!" Nancy screamed frantically. "Ned, are you all right?" But there was no response.

Chapter

Seventeen

N ED!" NANCY SCREAMED again. She listened for a response, and finally there was a faint murmuring coming from underneath the flat. But Nancy couldn't make out the words.

Nancy felt torn. Should she let Katya Alexandrovna go and run to help Ned? Or should she keep her grip on the dancer?

"All right, all right! What's going on here?" A police sergeant marched onto the stage. How did he get here? Nancy wondered. Trailing behind him were three officers, James Ellsworth, and—Brad.

The sergeant motioned to the flat. "Okay, pick that up," he ordered two of the policemen. Then he turned toward Nancy who was still holding Katya pinned to the floor. "Get those two on their feet," he told the third officer. "And make sure neither one gets away." Obviously, he wasn't sure which of them was the crook.

But Nancy didn't care. She was too worried about Ned. The police officers lifted the flat up.

Ned was lying on Colby, holding his arm behind his back in a wrestler's hold. Ned smiled over his shoulder. "Glad you dropped in," he told the police. "I was too busy holding on to this crook to push that flat away." He let go of Colby and then stood up.

Nancy was ready to run over and throw her arms around Ned, but she stopped herself in time. For a moment she had forgotten that they weren't a couple anymore.

Instead, Belinda walked over to Ned. Oh, no, Nancy thought, she's going to kiss him again. Do I really have to watch this?

But Belinda wasn't smiling. In fact, she looked so furious, she was practically green. "Ned Nickerson!" the dancer screamed. "I can't believe you've done this!"

Ned's eyebrows rose. "Wh-what?" he asked, completely confused.

"You've ruined the ballet! Of all the selfish,

horrible things to do! I never want to see you again. Ever!"

Nancy looked away, embarrassed for Ned. How could Belinda humiliate him in front of all those people. But, Nancy decided, it really made Belinda look bad. After all, she had just insulted the guy who'd captured the diamond thief!

As Belinda stalked off, the police sergeant approached Nancy. "Well, young woman, maybe you can explain what's going on here. This Brad fellow says you're the detective around here."

"Brad?" Nancy asked, turning to him. "How did you get involved in this?"

Brad stared at Nancy seriously. "When things started getting wild here, I went and called the police from the pay phone in the lobby." Then he muttered an afterthought. "That's what you should have done in the first place."

Nancy stared at Brad sadly. He still couldn't think of her as a detective, and she couldn't have fun with a guy who'd rather stay home and watch videos than jump into an adventure. Nancy frowned. Nice as Brad was, there wasn't anything between them. And she could tell that he felt the same way.

She knew for certain that she and Brad weren't going to be seeing each other in the future. She hoped they'd both find other people and maybe even stay friends, but she wouldn't really miss him as a boyfriend.

"Okay, let's have that explanation about what's going on here," the sergeant said, cutting in on her thoughts.

"It's simple, Sergeant. I've caught the thieves who stole the Raja diamond last week." She pointed first to Katya, then to Colby. "And what's more I've found the diamond itself."

"You're kidding," Brad gasped.

Murmurs of "amazing," and "I don't believe it," ran through the crowd.

"It's true. The pin was hidden in a pair of Katya's pointe shoes all along. The whole case became easy once I realized they were in the lost and found."

"Well, let's have it," the sergeant said.

But Ned was already walking over with the slippers tucked under his arm. He had held on to them all during the fight. He couldn't stop smiling. "How about letting Nancy reveal it," he said. He handed the shoes to her.

Nancy turned her concentration to the pink satin shoes. She unwrapped the ribbons, then stuck her hand into the toe of the first shoe. There was a wad of lamb's wool inside. But she could feel something hard beneath it. Slowly and with mounting excitement, she pulled out the pin with the Raja diamond. It sparkled brilliantly under the stage lights. It really was a magnificent gem!

Nancy turned to Katya. "Well, here's the proof. Your shoe with the diamond inside. I really hoped it wasn't you, Katya, but when it became clear that it was, I had no choice but to track you down."

Katya sighed. "It was a brilliant plan. And we would have gotten away with it, too, if you hadn't come snooping around. You almost got hurt very badly a few times during your investigation, and for that I really am sorry. We didn't want to hurt you but the closer you got to discovering us, the more necessary that became."

"Tell me if this is right. You planned the robbery for money and to get back at James for forcing you out. You figured the robbery would make a lot of problems for him and, in the end, discredit him as the managing director. You convinced Colby to help you because he was going to be out, too. And because he's so devoted to you."

"Yes," Katya admitted. "And James deserved it. He's ruining this ballet company. They shouldn't get rid of us, they should get rid of him!" She threw James a look of pure hatred.

"Colby attacked him the first day I was investigating just to throw suspicion on James," Nancy explained to the group.

"It's good that you're willing to confess," the sergeant said to Katya. "That ought to cut a few years off your prison term."

Nancy turned to Andre, who was standing with his arm around Ana. "So, you two were searching in the storage area for the diamond just to save

Ana's reputation and recover the jewel for the Rajas?"

Ana nodded.

James peered at her angrily. "You tore up the whole costume room just for that? Do you know how much damage you caused? It's going to take thousands of dollars to repair all those clothes!"

Nancy moved over and laid a hand on James's shoulder. "I've got one question for you. What job did Belinda do for you? At first, I thought it was the diamond robbery."

James glared. "Certainly not. It was a little fund-raiser I planned. She danced. That's all. Audiences love to watch her because she's so young and beautiful, so they buy more tickets. That's what's most important to me—the tickets."

"That's exactly your problem," Colby spat out. "You put no value on a great artist like Katya because she's a bit older."

James threw Colby a snide look, but he didn't answer him. "So now, with Katya out of the way, Belinda's career will really be able to take off. She'll be cast in all the major roles."

Nancy frowned. It really was sad that a fabulous dancer like Katya and a talented director like Colby would no longer be with the company. Nancy realized then that it didn't bother her anymore that Belinda was becoming a star now that things between her and Ned weren't going well.

Feeling better than she had in a few weeks, Nancy turned to Ned. "Thanks for helping me on this one, Ned. I couldn't have done it without you."

Ned grinned. "To tell you the truth, Nancy, it was fun—except for the part with the elevator shaft. Anyway, I think we should go out and celebrate a mystery well solved!"

Nancy laughed. "Sure. How about the River Heights Café tomorrow night."

"Our old favorite club for dancing," Ned mused nostalgically. "I couldn't have thought of a better idea myself." He put his arm around her shoulder. Then, despite the crowd of people watching, he bent down and kissed her gently on the cheek.

Nancy couldn't help but smile. "What was that for?" she asked, surprised.

A wide grin spread over Ned's face. "Just for old times' sake."

Nancy sighed happily. She was sure that kiss wasn't just for old times, but also for the beginning of good times ahead.

Nancy's Next Case:

Nancy Drew can't refuse a challenge. Especially when it involves murder.

It's an old case, but it reveals new surprises, including an amazing secret about Hannah Gruen. It also includes new dangers, as Nancy and Ned track down a person who's gotten away with murder for thirty years.

With each step, Nancy comes closer to the killer.

But is she also coming closer to her own death?

Find out the answer in *Buried Secrets,* Case #10 in The Nancy Drew Files™.

Have you seen
Nancy Drew
lately?

Nancy Drew has become a girl of the 80s! There is hardly a girl from seven to seventeen who doesn't know her name. Now you can continue to enjoy Nancy Drew in a new series, written for older readers – THE NANCY DREW FILES. Each book has more romance, fashion, mystery and adventure.

Join Nancy in all these fabulous adventures, available only in Armada.

ARMADA

Nancy Drew Mystery Stories

Nancy Drew is the best-known and most-loved girl detective ever. Join her and her best friends, George Fayne and Bess Marvin, in her many thrilling adventures available in Armada.

ARMADA

Stevie Day
Series

JACQUELINE WILSON

Supersleuth	£2.25	☐
Lonely Hearts	£2.25	☐
Rat Race	£2.25	☐
Vampire	£2.25	☐

An original new series featuring an unlikely but irresistible heroine – fourteen-year-old Stevie Day, a small skinny feminist who has a good eye for detail which, combined with a wild imagination, helps her solve mysteries.

"Jacqueline Wilson is a skilful writer, readers of ten and over will find the (Stevie Day) books good, light-hearted entertainment."

Children's Books December 1987

"Sparky Stevie" *T.E.S. January 1988*

ARMADA

All these books are available at your local bookshop or newsagent, or can be ordered from the publisher. To order direct from the publishers just tick the title you want and fill in the form below:

Name _____

Address _____

_____

Send to: Collins Childrens Cash Sales
          PO Box 11
          Falmouth
          Cornwall
          TR10 9EN

Please enclose a cheque or postal order or debit my Visa/Access –

Credit card no:

Expiry date:

Signature:

– to the value of the cover price plus:

UK: 60p for the first book, 25p for the second book, plus 15p per copy for each additional book ordered to a maximum charge of £1.90.

BFPO: 60p for the first book, 25p for the second book plus 15p per copy for the next 7 books, thereafter 9p per book.

Overseas and Eire: £1.25 for the first book, 75p for the second book. Thereafter 28p per book.

ARMADA